DIEGO'S CROSSING

ROBERT HOUGH

annick press
toronto + new york + vancouver

Edited by Barbara Pulling
Cover photo (red poppy) © Gabylastar/Dreamstime.com
Cover design by Diana Sullada
Chapter opening design © Transia Design

We thank Juan Adrián Pérez Yáñez of Autonomous University of Baja
California for his expert review.

Annick Press Ltd.

We acknowledge the support of the Canada Council for the Arts, the Ontario
Arts Council, and the Government of Canada through the Canada Book Fund
(CBF) for our publishing activities.

ONTARIO ARTS COUNCIL
CONSEIL DES ARTS DE L'ONTARIO
an Ontario government agency
un organisme du gouvernement de l'Ontario

Cataloging in Publication

Hough, Robert, 1963-, author
    Diego's crossing / written by Robert Hough.
Issued in print and electronic formats.
ISBN 978-1-55451-757-2 (bound).—ISBN 978-1-55451-756-5 (pbk.).—
ISBN 978-1-55451-758-9 (html).—ISBN 978-1-55451-759-6 (pdf)
    I. Title.
PS8565.O7683D53 2015   jC813'.6   C2015-900846-8
                                                 C2015-900847-6

Published in the U.S.A. by Annick Press (U.S.) Ltd.

Printed in Canada

ANCIENT FOREST ™
FRIENDLY

Visit us at: www.annickpress.com
Visit Robert Hough at: www.roberthough.ca

Also available in e-book format. Please visit
www.annickpress.com/ebooks for more details.
Or scan

MIX
Paper from
responsible sources
FSC® C004071

Para el gran país de México

1

◣◥◣◥◣◥

WE'RE ON THE TWO-LANE HIGHWAY running out of our village toward Nuevo Laredo. The sun is a smeary white light that bakes the inside of the car. The windows are open, and I'm blinking away fine bits of desert sand. We haven't even reached highway speed, and already the car is trembling like an old man's hands.

"Fourth," Papi yells. "Put it in fourth, *hijo!*"

The Datsun is light blue, though rust has eaten away the panels so every time you close the door, little flakes of red-brown flutter onto the toes of your boots. It backfires when you start it, coughing up clouds of blue-gray smoke, and then struggles to do the speed limit. When it's running, it makes a weird smell, like the engine is roasting coffee beans.

"You know I took your mother on our first date in this car," Papi is always telling me. "I'll keep it till it turns to dust."

In the meantime, he's taken the clutch apart and put it back together a half-dozen times, always insisting that it should work fine now. Yet it never does, and getting the transmission into gear requires a bit of magic, which Papi's teaching me today.

I reach toward the gearshift. The plastic knob split and fell off long ago, so the only thing to grab on to is a grooved piece of metal where another knob would go if we could find one. I press the clutch with my left foot, shift into neutral, and pump the clutch again. Now comes the hard part: you have to slowly move the gear lever until you feel where the teeth haven't quite opened all the way. Then you waggle the shift until the gear finds its way around the block in the mechanism. I try, and hear a loud noise that's halfway between a rattle and a screech.

"It's okay," Papi says. "Try again."

I nod. We've already lost so much speed that a truck full of day workers races by us, the driver honking his horn and the men in the back all pointing and laughing. I shift again, and this time when I get to that point when the shift doesn't do what it's supposed to, I give a quick wrist flutter, just like Papi showed me, and the clutch finally engages.

"Good!" he says with a smile. "You're getting it."

I bring the car back up to speed. It's shuddering and the motor is howling and the wind is screaming through the windows. All around us is sand and scrub and low spiky cacti. A desert eagle floats high above. We can just barely make out the blanket of smog that hangs over Nuevo Laredo. Our plan is to drive there and go to our favorite taco stand, the one where the owner, a young guy named Miguel, is famous for his tripe in a chipotle sauce.

"*Dios mio*," Papi says. "I've been dreaming about those tacos all day."

I press my foot a little harder on the accelerator. At first the Datsun speeds up, but then it starts to tremble, like it's about to fly into a hundred pieces. "You better slow down," says Papi. "This car … she's the one who decides how fast we go. Don't worry, we'll get there eventually."

I ease off just as we're entering a long, slow turn that circles one of the few hills in Coahuila state. After I round it, it'll be clear sailing all the way to Nuevo Laredo and Miguel's lunch stand. With any luck, we'll get there before the lineups start.

I round the bend and that's when I see the same truck full of day workers come to a full stop amid a group of seven or eight vehicles, most of them pickup trucks as badly rusted as our Datsun. I wrestle the gearshift into neutral and slow down. Papi says nothing, but from the corner of my eye I can see his jaw muscles gnaw beneath his stubbly bronze skin. I notice that my heart is beating hard, like I've just run a race.

Someone has strung a long white banner acros the highway. As I cruise to a stop, I make out what it says: *This is what happens to those who offend the double letter.*

The Datsun shakes and stalls.

There's a wall of people, standing and looking down. They're mostly laborers, sturdily built campesinos with dark skin and tattered ball caps; most of them look like they're from the south, where the people are built wider and lower to the ground. None of them are speaking. They're just standing still, heads tilted downward, looking.

"Diego, don't," says Papi.

We both sit in the car, waiting, until I can't bear it any longer. I get out and walk toward the line of men, Papi calling for me to come back. Once there, I stand on my toes, gazing over the shoulder of an older man wearing a flannel shirt with a rip in the shoulder.

Instantly, I wish I'd listened to Papi.

THERE ARE FIVE OF THEM on the roadway, hands tied behind their backs. Three are lying on their stomachs and two are on their sides, their legs drawn up to their chests. Three are obviously cartel members because they're wearing baggy jeans and their arms are covered in tattoos, while the other two look like regular people—they could be our neighbors back down in Corazón de la Fuente. I blink, half-thinking that when I open my eyes the dead men will have disappeared. They haven't, and I blink again. I can't look for more than a few seconds at a time, the scene coming at me in flashes of red and brown.

I hear Papi's footsteps, nearing.

"Ay no," he mutters, and I swallow away the stomach acid that's splashed up into my throat. "Ay no," he says again. The men are headless, their bloody neck stumps buzzing with flies.

We hear sirens. They're getting louder.

"Come on," says Papi. "We better go."

Without his saying it, I know our driving lesson is over. I hand him the keys and we climb in the old Datsun. Papi turns the ignition and the starting motor whirrs away. Papi is usually amused by the car's failings, but now he curses and slaps his palm against the steering wheel, a lock of hair falling over his forehead.

"Come *on*," he growls.

The car finally starts in a cloud of burning oil. He reverses

8

and turns around and we head back to our village. Neither of us speaks. Neither of us is hungry anymore.

After a while, Papi turns off the highway onto a little track that leads north to the river. It's probably a path used by migrants planning on swimming their way into the United States. For a minute, I think he's going to try to drive along the track, which would probably make the Datsun's suspension fall right out of the bottom of the car.

Instead, he stops and shuts the motor off. We both sit looking ahead—topping a stretch of green-brown scrub is a thin ribbon of muddy river, and beyond that is *el norte*. I hear Papi's breathing.

"Don't tell Mami what we saw today."

"She'll hear about it anyway."

"But she doesn't need to know you've had a look. You hear me, Diego?"

"I hear you."

The gas fumes creeping through the floor are making me feel queasy. Or maybe it's the images of those dead men scrolling through my head. Those fastened hands, swollen and bleached by the sun. All those flies, buzzing like they'd gone insane. Those circles of red-brown where the victims' heads should have been, each the same size around as the plates Mami uses to serve up lunch.

In a second I'm out of the car, throwing up my breakfast onto the desert floor. I cough a few times and wipe my mouth and get back in the car.

"You okay?"

"*Si,*" I say.

"I told you not to get out of the car."

"I should've listened."

We sit in silence for a few minutes. It's like we were part of it, just because we were there afterward. Just because we're from the country where things like that happen.

Papi points across the border. "None of this would happen if *that* country didn't like drugs so much."

I can't tell whether he's thinking or fuming. Likely both.

"You have to ask yourself," he finally says, "why people living in a country so wealthy and free of problems would do that to themselves. Do you understand it, Diego? Do you know why that could be?"

I don't answer.

Papi turns the ignition and we hear that grating *whirr whirr whirr* once again. For a second he gets that glassy, quivering look people get when they're about to start crying.

He doesn't though.

The motor catches and we drive back home.

2

▽△▽△▽△▽

"DIEGO!"

I open my eyes. I roll over and, like every morning, try to go back to sleep. It doesn't work. It's been two weeks since Papi and I saw those bodies. Lately, no matter how much sleep I get, I still feel tired.

"Diego!"

Mami is outside the curtain that separates the room I share with Ernesto from the rest of the house.

"Diego!" she calls again. "Do you know what time it is?"

I grunt something.

"Get up!" she shouts. "You can't just lie around all day doing nothing!"

I groan and stare up at the same ceiling I've looked at since I was a kid. Sometimes I think my whole life story is written on this ceiling. Every water stain is something that's happened, every spiderweb some event in code. Every crack in the plaster is a milestone I should remember, but can't.

I sit, swinging my legs over the edge of the hammock. Covering the window is a thin curtain lit red by the sun. Ernesto's hammock is on the other side of the room, and it hasn't been slept in for four nights. The only other thing in the room is the dresser the two of us share. Naturally, the top drawers are his, even though he's barely here anymore.

I pull on a pair of Levi's and a white T-shirt. In the main room of our little house, I sit at the kitchen table. Papi's at the other end of the room, reading a day-old newspaper in his favorite chair. *Massive Tunnel Found!* is the front-page headline. Below the photo is a blown-up quote by the police, saying a few million dollars' worth of drugs were confiscated, just waiting to find their way into the States.

"I've got *frijoles con huevo*," Mami says.

"I'm good," I tell her.

"You have to eat."

"My stomach's still asleep."

"Like the rest of you."

Mami puts a plate in front of me. The eggs, I know, are fresh—from outside I can hear our chickens clucking away. But the beans are warmed up from who knows how many meals ago. They smell strange and they look too dark, jet-black instead of bean colored. My stomach turns and I push my breakfast away.

Mami hears it skid against the table. "Diego! What are you doing?"

"Going out," I say, sliding back the chair.

"Well, take your father with you. Otherwise he'll just sit in his chair all day."

My mood worsens, as it always does when Mami's right about

something. Papi's reading one of those newspapers devoted to the deaths caused by the drug wars. He's always reading them, even though he says they're a national disgrace. But that's the way Papi is: he reads *la nota roja* just to prove to himself he's right about the way he sees the world.

Today the first page shows a photo of a U-shaped entranceway, crashing through the fireplace of some old woman's home across the border in Texas. Apparently, she was seventy-two years old, with no "previously known" connection to the cartels.

Papi lowers the paper. His eyes look tired. I wish he'd do more with his day, just like Mami wishes I'd do more with *my* day. But that's the thing about families. Everyone wishes everyone else would do things differently.

"Papi," I say. "How 'bout another driving lesson?"

The truth is, we haven't driven together since we saw those headless corpses, and I know he's going to find some excuse.

"Maybe," he says with a shrug. "But I need to get the motor looked at. All that smoke. I think it's the carburetor. So maybe not."

I look at Mami in a way that says, *You see? I tried, didn't I?*

She sighs, and takes my full plate to the counter. She wraps it with cellophane and puts it in our clanking little refrigerator. Then she starts washing the other plates, her slender back to me.

I stretch, yawn, and get up. Mami looks over her shoulder. "Where are you going?" she calls.

"Vincente's," I mutter, and with that I'm out of there.

OUR HOUSE IS ON A SIDE STREET near the smaller of the town's two plazas. In the middle is an ancient stone well that dried up

13

years ago. If you used it now, all you'd get is a bucket's worth of sand or maybe a dead vole. The mayor would probably dig up the well, since it gets in the way of traffic, but there's this stupid old superstition in our town: if you lower your head into the well and whisper your problems, you'll supposedly feel better. While hardly anyone pays any attention to that old myth anymore, once in a while I'll still see one of the town's grandmothers totter up, stick her craggy face inside, and start weeping.

I walk west toward the town's central plaza. It's a dusty square lined with paloverde trees and heavy wrought-iron benches. The plaza is ringed with houses like the one I live in, made from adobe and painted either light blue or pink. (Thank God ours is one of the blue ones.) On the northeast corner, there's an old Spanish-built church. It must've been nice once—it's got lots of stained glass—except the steeple was hit by a bomb a long time ago, during the Mexican revolution. Supposedly the top of the steeple fell into the street, taking the church's bell with it. When the war ended, no one had enough money or bricks to fix it, so someone just sealed it with mud and straw. Ninety years later, there's still no steeple and there's still no bell, so on Sunday mornings Father Augusto has to walk into the middle of the plaza, cup his hands around his mouth, and holler that his service is about to start.

Vincente lives on a lane that snakes west toward the edge of the town, near the remains of an old radio tower that some crazy gringo built in the 1930s. I go around the back of his house and tap on the window of his room. The laneway is covered with muck and bits of twisted metal. A trio of dogs, their teats stretched and peeling and red, are rooting through a bag of garbage.

14

I hear Vincente stir inside.

"*Nini*," I whisper.

Nini is a name we call each other. It stands for a young male who doesn't study or work—*ni estudia, ni trabaja*—and it isn't a compliment. In fact, I got so tired of Mami calling me a *nini* I started to use it myself, just to take that weapon away from her. After a bit, Vincente started using it too.

"That you, *nini*?" I hear him say.

"*Si*."

"*Que pasa*?"

"Get up."

"All right."

After a bit, Vincente appears in the laneway, rubbing sleep out of his eyes. Unlike me, he's tall and skinny, all elbows and knees and neck. In the background I hear his mami's faint voice: "Vincente! Vincente! Where are you going? Don't just hang around all day …"

He just rolls his eyes and says, "What do you want to do?"

"Don't know. You?"

He shrugs his shoulders. As usual, we walk back through town. There's an old mission just south of here, halfway between the town and the highway. It's quiet and windblown and it's where us *ninis* go to kill the day.

A hawk circles overhead. The air smells like roasting corn. I can hear a TV set mumbling away, probably one of those idiot *telenovelas* the old people like so much. We reach the edge of the desert and as we walk toward the mission the sound of the television fades.

"Hey," he says. "You hear? They found a drug tunnel about

15

twenty minutes from here."

"Yeah."

"The thing was *huge*, *primo*. The length of four football fields. As wide as your house too. It had electric lights and a kitchen, along with a few million dollars' worth of drugs, piled up right in the middle of the thing. They're not even sure if the drugs were on the American or Mexican side. Either way, someone's going to be really pissed now that the police have shut it down."

I nod again, though really I'm ignoring him. It's all everyone talks about—the *narcoguerra* and the failing economy and the immigration fence, *blah blah blah*, as if this country has no room for good news anymore. Sometimes I think it's the reason my head feels so sludgy these days. It's all the news, making me feel like I can't think straight.

Dusty steps lead up to the mission. After four centuries, there isn't much of it left. Just three roofless vaults, the walls of each sprayed with graffiti. Five years ago, all those scribbles were who loved who and who'd broken up with who, along with logos of gringo bands like Nirvana and Korn. Lately, the graffiti has been changing. Now it's gang tags, the most common around here being two letter *C*s linked together.

Vincente and I sit at the top of the steps. We're both seventeen years old and there's nothing, not one thing, going on in our lives.

"Remember that *chica* we met at the party last Saturday?" Vincente asks. "Rosita?"

I nod.

"I was talking to her friend. You know, the one who works at the bakery?"

"Uh-huh."

"She says Rosita's way into you, *primo*."

"Oh."

"Oh! What do you mean 'oh'? She's *bien buena*, that one."

I shrug.

"I don't get you, *nini*."

"I'm not asking you to."

We look out over the town. It's called Corazón de la Fuente —"Heart of the Fountain"—which is ridiculous because there's no fountain, and when the water service fails, we have to carry sloshing pails from a row of pumps out near the cemetery.

A warm wind is blowing. It dries our skin and makes our lips feel dry. I wish we had something to drink. Cold *cerveza* or Coca-Cola or whatever. Everything's quiet except for the sound of huisache needles blowing over the mission. There's a *caw* from somewhere far away and the smell of burned corn in the air. It's all so exhausting I feel like going home and taking a nap. Of course, Mami would be all over me for being lazy, so I have no choice but to stay here and listen to Vincente go on and on about Rosita and how she may or may not like me.

We both hear something. For a second, I mistake it for thunder —not the kind that claps hard, but the kind that rumbles in the distance for seconds at a time before trailing away. The sound gets louder and I realize I'm listening to the muffled bass of a car stereo going *thump thump thump*.

I look toward the highway.

"*Órale!*" says Vincente. "You see that?"

A brand-new truck is turning onto the dirt road leading to our village. As soon as it makes the turn it slows. I figure the driver is worried about all that sand and gravel ruining the finish.

"What a ride!" Vincente says. "I wonder whose it is."

I shake my head, even though I know there's only one person it could possibly belong to.

3

▲▽▲▽▲▽

VINCENTE JUMPS UP and starts walking back along the path from the mission toward the center of town. I follow him, even though I'd just as soon stay up at the mission. The whole time we can hear the *thump thump thump* of the truck's sound system. Our neighbors are already opening their doors and stepping into the street and looking at each other with *qué pasa?* expressions. Little kids are holding their hands over their ears and hopping in one spot.

The truck enters the lane surrounding the plaza. Even through the tinted windows I can see my brother's smug expression, the one saying he doesn't care if he's bothering an entire town full of people so long as they're looking at him. He circles the plaza. The bass is so loud the truck's frame is vibrating along with it, the *thump thump thump* accompanied by the whine of trembling metal.

I don't know if Ernesto has borrowed the truck, bought it, or stolen it. With him, all three are possible. My stomach turns. It's

19

the idea that he has *this*, while Papi is stuck with a twenty-year-old Datsun.

It's a gun-gray Silverado with airbrushed Día de los Muertos figures across the door panels. There's chrome on the door handles, the mirror caps, the gas tank covers, and the nerf bars, the truck reflecting so much light it's shining. Judging by the numbers written on the side, it's got a 5.7 liter V-8, which means it must go like hell. Skeletons dance across the flatbed hutch.

My brother pulls up to Vincente and me and shuts off the motor. The sudden quiet is a relief. The plaza is flooded with people, all pointing and gawking and saying, *Is that Ernesto Hernandez? Is that his truck?* I breathe deeply, my fingers jittering at my sides.

There's a *whoosh* as the driver's side window lowers.

"Well, *hermano*?" Ernesto asks with a grin. "What do you think?"

I don't answer. I don't need to, since everyone else is talking at once: *Ay Ernesto!* and *Where'd you get that mad truck, cabrón?* and *Oye, primo, what a badass ride!*

Still, he's staring right at me.

"I'm asking you, Diego. What do *you* think?"

I shrug like I couldn't care less. Ernesto chuckles and looks at the others who've come up.

"You want to see something?" he asks them.

"Ay, *sí!*" says the crowd.

Ernesto grins again, the diamond set into his front tooth glinting in the sunlight. He flips a switch on the dash and the lane turns purple beneath him.

"*Órale!*" groans Vincente. "That is pure loco, Ernesto!"

"You should see it at night!"

The village men run their hands over the finish and bend to admire the jacked chassis and dual tires. Some of the señoras are coming out as well, and start to cluck about Ernesto and what he's come home with. Mami, of course, is with them. She's wearing a threadbare old dress that's wet in the front from dishwater, and even though this is pretty much what the other señoras are wearing, I feel embarrassed for her.

"Ernesto!" she screams. "You're home!"

He steps out and she runs into his arms, giving him a dozen kisses on his cheeks, chin, and neck. "Mami!" he says with a laugh. "Take it easy, you'll break me in two!"

"Hey, Ernesto," calls one of the men. "Pop the hood!"

Ernesto does, and the men crowd around the motor, oohing and aahing like it's the Second Coming of Christ. "Ernesto!" calls a pretty *chica* in a tight white blouse. "Open the other windows!" Ernesto lowers them with the same soft *whoosh*. Pretty soon, a half dozen teenagers—Vincente included—are leaning into the truck, admiring the leather.

"My, my," a friend of Mami says to Ernesto. "That job of yours in Laredo must be working out well!"

Ernesto gives a bashful grin, and says, "Oh, it is," and everyone laughs like it's the funniest thing anyone's ever said.

It seems like half the town has come out to see Ernesto and his new truck. One exception is Papi. No matter how hard I scan the crowd, I can't find him, and the only thing I can think is he's still inside, reading his *nota roja* and brooding.

Mami is laughing and joking with the neighbors, her face flushed like she's won a prize. Someone's grandmother shows up with bottles of pop, and starts selling them for five pesos. The hot dog man, Alejandro, wheels his little red wooden cart into the plaza, happy to have a crowd to sell hot dogs to. Attached to the cart is a little crank handle. When he turns it, it plays the Frito Bandito song.

This impromptu gathering goes on and on, the crowd breaking off into groups of three and four. Ernesto is outside of the truck, moving from group to group, asking people how they're doing and what they've been up to. He tells the older señoras that if they need help with anything—fetching groceries, moving furniture—he'd be pleased to help them while he's home. They smile and thank him, even though everyone knows it'll never happen. That's the difference between Ernesto and me. If *I* made a promise I didn't follow through on, I'd hear about it forever. But with my older brother? With him it doesn't matter. It's like he's done enough already, just by talking to them.

He glares at me. I swear, it's like he can read my thoughts. He comes over, suddenly looking all serious. In our family, Papi is stocky, Mami the opposite. Since Ernesto takes after Mami, he's leaner than me and not nearly as broad in the shoulders. With his tattoos and hairnet and baggy gangster pants, people think he's tougher than me. I know the truth, though, and that makes him loco.

His grin appears out of nowhere. Funny how everyone else thinks it's friendly but to me it's a threat.

"Take a ride, *hermano*."

"I'm busy."

"Like hell you're busy."

"I told Papi I'd help him with something."

22

"What would you help *him* with? Turning the pages of his *nota roja*? I said take a ride, *pendejo*."

"Can't."

"Yes you can, Diego ..." And it goes on and on this way, with Ernesto pestering me and pestering me until I give up and get in the passenger seat. Vincente, who's been watching the whole exchange, narrows one eye at me and cocks his thumb while pointing his index finger at me, like his hand is a little gun. Then he grins.

Meanwhile, Ernesto is kissing Mami, saying he's just going to take me for a quick ride, that the two of us have something to talk about.

"Well, don't be gone long, *hijo*. I'm making your favorite tonight."

There's music coming from somewhere, playing over the drone of Alejandro's hot dog cart, and men are opening bottles of Tecate and Dos Equis. Ernesto and I pull away, driving slowly along the laneway leading out of town. When we reach the paved highway, he floors the accelerator. There's a roar and my head hits the headrest behind me. The broken line in the middle of the road turns into a blurred yellow streak. He lifts his foot off the pedal and the motor calms. Really, we could be parked it's so quiet. I peek at the dashboard.

Dios mio, I think. We're doing a hundred and forty kilometers an hour. So *this* is driving.

I'm looking out a tinted window, over scrubland crowded with mesquite and prickly pear. Everything seems kind of blue and unreal, like we're on some cold, distant planet.

"Diego," he says.

Don't start, I think.

"Diego," he says again. "I had a talk with Mami before I left the last time."

You always do, I think.

"Listen, *cabrón*. I know how it is here. Not a job for a thousand miles, unless of course you count the border factories where they'll pay you eighty cents an hour if you're lucky. And who's got money for college? All those books and travel and what all else. I know how you feel. Like you got no options. Like you don't know why you should even bother getting up in the morning. It happens."

I keep looking out the window. I can't believe Ernesto expects me to take him seriously, what with the way he makes his money.

"All I can say is you got to stay positive. You gotta have *faith*, *cabrón*." He's gesturing now, and I can tell he's enjoying this little talk. It's making him feel important and wise, which is such a disgusting thought I can't help but speak up.

"So I should do what you do?"

"I didn't say that. But I'll tell you one thing. You don't see me lying around all day, doing nothing. No matter what, you gotta live."

He's smacking the steering wheel with his palm, like he's in line at a drive-through and the wait is driving him nuts. That's when I look over and notice he's got a new tattoo, high up on the right side of his neck. I swallow hard.

"What're you looking at, *hermano*?"

"Nothing."

"Yeah, you are. You're looking at something."

24

"I'm not."

"Don't you judge me, Diego."

"I won't."

"I get enough from Papi."

"Maybe you deserve it."

He slams on the brakes. We drop to zero in a matter of seconds. *Damn*, I think. Not an inch of slide or sway. He looks at me and I refuse to look back.

"Get out."

This grabs my attention. We're in the middle of the desert. You could die of thirst or snakebite out here.

"No."

"Get out."

"You get out."

"Get out *now*."

Stepping into the baking heat, I'm surprised when Ernesto gets out as well. Yet I'm not surprised by what follows: he charges around the truck, coming in low and hard. He hits me around the waist and takes me down, dirtying my jeans and white T-shirt. The blood pumping through my limbs feels good. We're rolling around in the earth, and since he got the jump on me I'm keeping him tight to me so he can't strike. We roll over two or three times and I throw him away, and then we're both on our feet, ready to spar.

We circle each other, and every time Ernesto throws a punch I duck or sidestep it easily. We've been fighting this way since we were kids, though ever since I grew bigger than him I've had the advantage. The strange thing is, now that I can kick his ass he seems to enjoy our fights even more.

He takes another swing, and when he blocks my counter he leaves a side of his face so wide open a grandmother could connect. I pop him one hard, right in the eye, and he bends over, holding himself and laughing.

"*Hijo de puta*! You really got me."

"You started it."

"You punch like Mike Tyson. Ow!"

He walks bent over, in little circles, holding his eye and giggling. After a bit, he straightens and lights a Marlboro. He hands me one. I don't smoke but I light it anyway. It's just the two of us, leaning against the truck. A wind comes up and blows ash off our cigarettes and disintegrates in the heavy air. For some reason, I feel better than I have in weeks. It's like hitting Ernesto thinned out some of the cobwebs in my head.

"Listen to me, Diego. It's not what you think. I'm an errand boy, nothing more. Strictly low level. I'll be rich in a year or two and then I'll get out of it."

I shrug, like I don't care one way or another.

Already, Ernesto's thin face is starting to swell; by nightfall he'll have a pretty decent shiner. He puts his right hand to it, pressing the puffiness with his fingertips. "You know what the worst part is?" he asks. "Everyone in town is going to know you did this."

It's true. He'll take a lot of ribbing over this one. I can't help it. I start grinning for the first time in weeks. The sun is hot on our faces and all the sand we kicked up has settled in our mouths and throats. The middle knuckle on my right hand hurts and I'm wondering whether I jammed it. If so, it'll swell like Ernesto's face.

"Listen, Diego. You need money or whatever, you ask me. But you gotta stop being so mopey or Mami's going to go crazy. She worries, is all. Mothers are like that. She doesn't want you turning out like Papi. She doesn't need two men in her life who've given up."

"Don't say that about Papi."

We both shut up and turn our faces toward the blue sky. The sun bakes our faces. I feel a throbbing behind my ribs, like he somehow punched my insides when I wasn't looking.

Yes, there are many times I hate my brother. But for some reason this isn't one of them.

4

⟁⟁⟁⟁

THE SUN BEGINS TO DIP, the desert turning a light purple. The sky fills with bats and nighthawks. Ernesto parks just outside our house, his truck blocking the lane. Any other drivers now have to go all the way around the plaza.

Mami comes rushing out.

"Ay! *Hijo!* What happened to your eye?"

Ernesto laughs and points to me. "I was teaching Diego a lesson."

Mami glares at me. "Diego! Did you do this?"

I'm tempted to say that Ernesto started it but I don't. Already she's turned her back and is leading Ernesto inside the house, her slender hand on his elbow. From the back, they look so similar: same walk, same build, same angle of the head.

"I've made your favorite," she coos. "*Chiles en nogada!*"

"Really?" says Ernesto. "Ay, *gracias*, Mami. I've been looking forward to your cooking all week."

I follow them inside and sit with Ernesto on our battered sofa.

Papi lowers his newspaper and nods at Ernesto, as if his son has just stepped out for a few minutes instead of four full days. Mami brings over a plate of quesadillas, saying we must be hungry and this will tide us all over. Ignoring the food, Papi gets up to fetch himself a beer.

"Hey, Papi," Ernesto says. "I'll have one as well."

Papi sighs before handing his eldest son a Tecate. Then he sits back down and hides behind his opened newspaper.

See the Ferocious Way He Bled is the headline.

The official story is that Ernesto has a construction job in Nuevo Laredo, filling in for workers who've gone on vacation or sick leave. When he gets called in, he supposedly goes to Laredo and works around the clock, making mad *dinero* with all the hours. The rest of the time, he's at home. It's a ridiculous story. There isn't a construction job in all of Mexico that'll pay for a customized Silverado. Still, if you walked up to my *mami*, and told her the truth about Ernesto—if you told her what was obvious to everyone in Corazón de la Fuente but her—she'd slap your face and accuse you of being jealous of Ernesto's success.

Mami calls us to the table. We sit and join hands. Ernesto says grace: "Thank you, O Lord, for this gift of food, which we are about to receive with gratitude and humility. Amen."

He looks up, smiling. The good feeling I had about him in the desert vanishes, along with any appetite I might've had.

Ernesto digs in, taking huge mouthfuls of pepper and rice and beans, washing it all down with glugs of Tecate. His hair is gelled and combed back from his forehead. Tattoos cover his arms and shoulders. Every time I see him, he has another. They bloom up the side of his neck now, like a dark green vine. They seep from beneath his scoop-neck T-shirt, half covered by white cotton and half exposed to the room's dim light. I can see the head of a growling tiger. The scythe of the Grim Reaper. Roses. Crosses. The name of one of his old girlfriends. I know he's working on a big hearse across his back; I can see the roofline only, like a deathly horizon. High on his neck, surrounded by moons and stars, is the tattoo that bothers me the most.

A pair of linked *C*s.

Mami notices I'm not eating. You can see the thoughts running through her head. Sometimes the muscle beneath her left eye twitches and now is one of those times. I know why. She's asking herself whether she should concern herself with her moody son Diego or whether she should let it go and enjoy her other son's return. She's actually stopped in mid-chew, a grain of rice on her lips.

I look down. My stomach churns. No one other than your mother can make you feel this way.

"Mami!" says my brother. "It's delicious! Everything is perfect."

She grins and rubs Ernesto's back in little circles.

"Do you want me to make more rice, *hijo*?"

"Ay no. There's already enough to feed the national football team."

Mami laughs like it's the funniest thing she's ever heard. It's not even true. She's made the same amount of food she always makes. Still, there are the two of them, giggling like muchachas at a party. Papi gets up and moves back to his chair.

"So," Mami says to Ernesto. "You're staying in tonight?"

"Ay no, Mami. I've got a party to go to." He gives her a disappointed look that is pure theater. In fact, sometimes I think

Ernesto *should* be an actor—there's a force that comes off him. He's like Heath Ledger as the Joker, or that crazy killer in *Seven*. When he's in a room, everyone can't help but keep their eyes on him, whether they want to or not. It's weird to say, I know, but the thing I hate most and the thing I admire most about my brother are the same.

My mother looks crestfallen. "But you just got back."

"I know, I know," Ernesto says with a dumb what-can-I-do-about-it smile.

"Where's the party?" Papi asks from behind his *nota roja*.

"In Laredo."

"Is Violeta going?" Mami asks.

"Mami, you know I stopped seeing her!"

"Good!" she exclaims. "I told you she was no good, that woman."

"And did I listen or not?" He grins at her. "Don't I always do what I'm told?"

"Still … you be careful."

"I always am," he says, which is the lie of the century. He couldn't be careful if someone offered him a million dollars.

For dessert, we eat flan and drink grainy coffee. Ernesto kisses Mami, thanks her again, and then heads for our bedroom, leaving his messy plate and napkin and a crumpled beer can for her to clean up. Mami clears the dishes while Papi turns on our fuzzy black-and-white TV to watch a football game from Mexico City.

I sit and watch as well, though it's difficult to hear the TV over Ernesto humming away in our bedroom. Ten minutes later, he comes out looking pretty much like he did before, only he's changed into a pair of jeans that are slightly baggier and lower slung than the ones he had on when we fought in the desert. I watch as he goes to Mami and kisses her on the cheek.

"*Hasta luego*, Mami."

Then he slips some gringo dollars in Mami's apron pocket, saying, "Here's a little something ..." He even glances at Papi, as if to say, *This is the way things are now.*

"*Gracias*, Ernesto," Mami replies. "You're a good son."

Papi keeps his eyes fixed on the game, gnashing his jaw muscles beneath his skin, his stare so hard you know he's barely seeing the players rush around in front of him.

Ernesto steps outside and I hear the motor of his new truck start up. Like before, he tours slowly around the village plaza before heading toward the road leading to the highway. When I hear him gun the engine, I know he's reached pavement.

I sit watching television with Papi. Saltillo has scored against the team from Distrito Federal, and even though Saltillo is my father's team he doesn't react. He just sits there, silent, devouring some space well beyond the television with his eyes. In the background, Mami scrubs the evening's dishes.

Ten minutes later, I hear someone knocking at the door. I hop up and throw it open and there's Vincente, all six and a half feet of him, looking happy and impatient and like he only wants to get going.

"*Nini!*" he says. "Where you *been*, *cabrón*?"

5

△▽△▽△▽

OUR AMIGO FERNANDO lives in the northeast corner of town, in a house near a ruined hacienda that used to belong to some rich Spanish landowner type. Supposedly, the hacienda got wrecked during the revolution so the guy hightailed it back to Spain, leaving his big house empty. Part of the roof is missing, one of the walls has been replaced by plastic sheeting, and it's filled with migrant families from Guatemala and El Salvador—they cram into the old house and squat there before crossing into *el norte* with everything they own on their backs.

"*Qué pasa, ninis?*" Fernando asks when he comes to the door. He doesn't look surprised to see us.

Having failed biology last year, Fernando is doing a makeup course so technically he's not a *nini* or at least he's not one yet. For now, the only reason his parents aren't bugging him to make something of his life is because he was too lazy to do his homework. If I'd known how much aggravation it would've saved me, I would've failed biology as well.

"*Qué onda?*" asks Vincente.

"Nothing. You?"

"Nothing."

The three of us walk across town. Soon we're following the path through the desert, heading toward the steps leading up to the mission. We're not alone. It's a Saturday night, and already there are three or four groups of young people up there, drinking beer and talking. Everyone nods at us and then we sit and look out over the city.

Fernando pulls a fifth of tequila from his inside jacket pocket. He spins off the top and takes a long slug.

"Pass it here," Vincente says, his hand extended.

Fernando hands the bottle to Vincente, who takes a long swallow. "Ay *caray*," Vincente says. "It's got a kick to it."

"You're telling me."

Vincente passes the bottle to me; it smells like a mix of kerosene and dead leaves. The small sip I take burns the back of my throat.

"That all you're going to have?" asks Vincente. "You know, you drink like an old woman."

I shrug. Two weekends ago, I drank a bunch of *cervezas* at a party and it put me in a mood I thought I'd never get out of. When the bottle comes my way again I have another sip, this one just big enough to satisfy Vincente.

Vincente and Fernando kill the rest of the bottle. Though I wouldn't say they're drunk, they're laughing and talking loudly about football and all the *chicas* they like. As darkness falls, people start leaving the mission and wending their way back into town, looking for a party.

We do the same, because that's what you do in Corazón. You collect your best friends, you go up to the mission, you get drunk, and then you drift back down to the plaza once the families have finished their after-dinner stroll. If you're older and you have a car, you might go to Laredo or Juárez or Piedras Negras. But when you're seventeen and stuck in Corazón, you do the same thing every Saturday. A lump rises in my throat and I feel tempted to tell Vincente and Fernando I've got an ache in my stomach so I can go home and keep Papi company. Instead I keep walking, head down, hoping they won't notice my mood.

Which they don't. They're going on and on about some *chica* in Fernando's remedial biology class named Laura. Apparently she just moved to Corazón from Zacatecas.

"Ay *primo*," Fernando's saying. "You should see how beautiful she is!"

"Tell me."

"Green eyes, *primo*!"

"No."

"You should see them! Like jade marbles. You ever seen that, *nini*?"

"In the movies, maybe, but not in Corazón de la Fuente."

"I hope she's out tonight. You can see for yourself. I'd *kill* for a girl with green eyes!"

There are about twenty or thirty kids at the plaza, all standing around in little groups, some in the light thrown by wrought-iron lampposts while others settle in pockets of darkness.

Fernando's there for one reason and one reason only, and that's to hunt for the green-eyed siren from his biology class. Vincente, however, wants to socialize, and as we pass each group he stops to talk and catch up. Fernando and I fidget and look around.

A guy named Pedro who used to be in my shop class comes up and says, "Hey Diego? Where's your brother? That's some truck he's driving these days."

"You've got that right," someone else says. "That ride of his is way cool."

Pretty soon, another three or four people drift over and start talking about my brother. My mood is now even worse than it was five minutes ago. It might seem like they're gabbing about Ernesto's truck, but what they're really talking about is the fact that he's made it into the Coahuilan Cartel. No one ever says it out loud, but it's what people mean when they say, *I wonder where that mad cabrón got the money.* Or, *I never knew construction paid so much!* Or, *Where do I go for a job interview?*

I'm feeling tenser by the minute. Vincente notices and comes to the rescue.

"Anyone here seen that new girl, Laura?" he asks. "Fernando will go crazy if he doesn't find her soon."

Everyone laughs and Fernando turns red. We move off. You can tell Fernando's pissed at Vincente, though he brightens when he spots Laura toward one corner of the plaza, standing in a clump of other *chicas*.

"There she is," he gasps. "There she is … what do I do?"

"Go talk to her," says Vincente.

"What if I make a fool of myself?"

"You already have, *cabrón*."

Fernando thinks. "You're right."

"So go."

"I don't know …"

"Go, *primo*."

Fernando takes a deep breath and marches off. Vincente laughs.

"You think he has a chance?" I ask him.

"Not in a million years. She can have any guy she wants."

People are starting to clear away from the plaza. We run into a few muchachos we know from school. Their names are Antonio and Felix. They're both a little drunk.

"*Que pasa?*" Vincente asks them.

Antonio answers. "You know Rosita Valasquez?"

"The one who likes Diego?"

"*Claro.* Her parents have gone to Piedras to visit an aunt or something. Everyone's heading over there."

Rosita's house is just down the street from the municipal cemetery. Apparently, the infant grandniece of some leader from the Mexican revolution is buried there. I have no idea what she was doing in a place like Corazón de la Fuente when she died, and I can't remember the name of the revolutionary leader—Carranza or Carranata or something like that. Still, it's the town's one claim to fame, and every once in a while some history buff shows up to look at the grave while tapping notes into an iPad. Supposedly, the coffin is the size of a hatbox.

When we get to Rosita's house, it's full of people. Norteño music is blasting on a crappy boom box. I notice Fernando way over in a corner, and I have to hand it to him: he's standing close to green-eyed Laura, who's laughing at everything he says. Vincente sees someone he knows and moves off. It's noisy and hot and crowded. What I wouldn't give to live in an actual city, with different things to do and different people to look at. Someone

37

passes me a bottle of mescal and this time, I take a good long swig. It goes down burning. Instantly, my brain warms and I don't have the energy to think as hard as I did before.

I pass the bottle on, and that's when I spot Rosita coming toward me, smiling bashfully. Vincente and Fernando are right, I suppose. She's wearing a snug polka-dot dress and bright red lipstick and a bright orange flower in her hair. I can tell she spent some time putting herself together, and I hope she didn't do it for me. The strange thing is, I used to think about chicas all the time. I used to find it hard to concentrate in class, just because they were there, chatting and giggling and putting on lip gloss and batting eyelashes heavy with mascara. But lately, ever since I started feeling tired all the time—since my head started feeling like it was filled with hotcake batter—they seem to have stepped away from my brain. In some ways it's a relief, but at the same time I wonder if there's something wrong with me.

"*Hola*, Diego," she says.

"*Hola*."

"When did you get here?"

"Just now."

There's an awkward pause. She walked up to me so I know I should do my part by being friendly. There's a hundred things I could say. I could ask when she expects her parents are coming home and whether they're okay with her having this fiesta. Or I could ask how her brother's doing—he's a year older and I used to play football with him before he went away to university in the capital. Or I could tell her how nice she looks, which is true, she really does look pretty, though I can't seem to get excited about her tonight. But I don't say anything. The ache has returned to my throat and so I just stand there, big and stupid, Rosita clamping her lip between her teeth.

Suddenly she brightens. "Diego, would you like to dance?"

"All right."

She takes my upper arm and leads me into one of the bedrooms, which they've cleared of hammocks so it serves as a dance floor. Los Tigres del Norte are blaring and everyone seems to be having a good time and so I try, I really do, and every few seconds Rosita leans forward and yells up at me, though with the music blaring off the walls and the din of all those voices, it's tough to hear so I just smile like an idiot. The truth is I've never liked norteño music; I wish it was Metallica or Linkin Park or maybe some old-school Sabbath, but no. It's Los Tigres singing about some perfect girl in some perfect place and how pretty and *linda* everything is. It's enough to make me sick. The truth is, it's been years since Los Tigres have even lived in Mexico, and if they moved back I wonder whether they'd still find everything *linda* enough to sing about.

I'm about to tell Rosita I want some air when a slow song comes on. Enrique Iglesias, for Christ's sake. Again, she looks up at me with her big brown eyes and I'm starting to think she really did doll herself up for *me* tonight. I open my arms and she holds me so close I can feel her warm breath on my neck. She smells of perfume and lime and nothing else. Unlike most of the other chicas, she doesn't talk a lot or drink a lot or smoke cigarillos, and that's why everyone says we're meant for each other: she's the only girl in high school who's serious enough to put up with me. We sway to the music. All around us, couples are kissing and slipping hands inside each other's clothing. I don't know why, but an image of those bodies that Papi and I saw flashes in front of my eyes. Suddenly, the floor sways beneath my feet and it feels like the mescal in my stomach is starting to froth.

Rosita looks up and notices. Her eyes widen with concern. "Diego, are you all right?"

"*Si* ... I mean ... no, I think I could use some air."

"Do you want to go outside?"

"*Si*," I say, thinking I'll leave her and she'll dance with someone else and that'll be the end of it. Instead, she takes my hand and leads me into cool desert air. We keep walking, the sky above us filled with silver light. When the sounds of the party are distant and low she stops. It's cool out here and if I had a jacket I'd give it to her.

"Are you feeling better?" she asks.

"*Si* ... sometimes I get a little uncomfortable in crowds."

She moves closer. "I do too," she says, and I know I'm supposed to put my arms around her. So I do. A second later she tilts her face up and lightly touches her lips to mine. I can feel her hands on the small of my back. After a few seconds, her lips part, though when the tip of her tongue slips inside of my mouth I feel like it's happening to someone else. I feel like I'm barely even there.

She pulls away. "Diego," she says.

"*Si*?"

"I'm a good girl. You do know this, don't you?"

I nod.

"So before this goes any further you have to promise me something."

"All right."

"Promise me that this means something to you. Promise me that you really care for me."

Last year, five girls in her class got engaged and who knows how many have followed suit this summer. So before we go any further, I'm supposed to say, *Ay Rosita, te quiero, te amo, you're the one for me*, and without even closing my eyes I can picture every minute of my future that would come of it, each day exactly the same as the one before it.

"I'm sorry," I tell her.

Her eyes widen with disbelief. Other muchachos would've just lied, and no one knows this more than Rosita. Maybe that's what she wanted.

"I'm sorry," I tell her again.

"I see," she says, gazing down at the sand. For some reason, I think of all the snakes and scorpions that live in the desert. I have an impulse to warn her, to tell her that they're all down there, crawling around at her feet, only she can't see them because it's dark.

"Diego," she says in a breaking voice. "I'd like you to go home now."

"All right."

Without looking up, she turns and walks back toward her house, her arms wrapped around herself. I look up at the sky. It's crowded with stars and a fat round moon and backing it all is a thin white milky wash.

There's no reason, I think. *There's no reason for anything at all.*

6

⩗⩗⩘⩗⩘⩗

WHEN I GET HOME, Papi and Mami are in bed and Ernesto is still out. I tiptoe to my room and climb into my hammock. I can hear the distant gurgle of the party, though after a bit it stops: most likely the neighbors complained. A few of my school friends stumble past our house, talking loudly about every dumb subject under the sun. Then everything goes quiet. My ears start making their own noise, a high-pitched whistle caused by too much thinking. I can't sleep. The minutes pass like dripping glue. I get up and have some quesadillas and then I go back to bed, my mind still churning madly and still I just lie there, staring up at the darkened ceiling, imagining every crack and stain.

I keep checking the clock radio on the dresser I share with Ernesto. It's like being at a job you don't like, though instead of waiting for break time or lunchtime, you're waiting for your exhaustion to defeat whatever it is that's keeping you awake. Around two o'clock in the morning, I hear something. At first I figure it's yet another noise thrown up by my worried mind.

But after a minute or so, when it continues to build in volume, I realize it's a car or truck, driving in from the highway. It's not Ernesto because the driver is charging through the streets, the engine growling like an enraged lion. You can hear the little chips and stones bouncing off the vehicle's body, something my brother would never have allowed.

I leap out of bed and pull on my jeans and boots. I've just made it outside the house when a white late-model Tahoe exits the plaza and tears up our street. It's pimped out like Ernesto's truck, with custom chrome, a hand-designed grill, and tinted windows. Instead of dancing skeletons, airbrushed lightning bolts span the door panels.

The Tahoe stops in front of our house beneath a street lamp. There are three guys in the truck, all with tattoos and gold chains around their necks. I don't know the driver or the one on the passenger side. But Ernesto is in the middle and he doesn't look good. His eyes are closed and his head is lolling against the back of the seat. The skin of his face looks loose, like something's happened to the muscles underneath.

The passenger door opens. One of the guys jumps out and takes Ernesto beneath the arms. Ernesto moans lightly as he's dragged out of the truck. The driver sits in the cab, looking forward, smoking a cigarette. He's wearing a mesh hairnet, like the ones dishwashers wear in gringo restaurants.

The man drops Ernesto at my feet. The stranger has a tattoo on his face, teardrops falling from his right eye. He looks straight at me.

"You his brother?"

"*Si.*"

"Crazy *vago* was racing his truck on the highway. There was an accident. The Silverado's history, *primo*."

I just stare at Ernesto.

"He's your problem now," the guy says before jumping back into the Tahoe. The pair calmly drive away as Ernesto writhes at my feet. I crouch down. My heart's pounding.

"Ernesto," I whisper. "Can you hear me?"

He groans. Though I can't see any cuts or bruises, I know he's hurt badly.

"*Hermano*," I say. "What happened?"

His eyes open. The weak light thrown from the lampposts seems to cause him extra pain.

He winces and says, "Diego, it's my head."

"You hit it?"

"*Sí, sí.*"

"How?"

"It's gone … the truck's gone …"

He's breathing heavily. He groans with each lungful of dusty air.

"Diego." He grunts. "You gotta get me inside … before Mami …"

"Can you move your arms and legs?"

"*Sí* … please, help me up … it's my head, really … I'm too dizzy to walk by myself …"

I bend over and slip an arm under his right shoulder.

"Okay, you ready? One, two, three."

I stand and Ernesto straightens his legs. With his body leaning against mine, I walk him into the house, trying to get him into his hammock before Mami wakes and freaks out completely.

It's too late. She's heard the noise and comes out in her night-gown, a hand covering her wide-open mouth. It's like she can't make a sound; all she can do is stand there, tears welling in her eyes, whimpering slightly.

Papi follows her out in his sad thin cotton pajamas. When he sees Ernesto he instantly understands that something terrible has happened. Unlike Mami, who looks like she's losing her mind, he just takes a deep breath and stands there. Really, it's like he's been expecting this all along.

"Papi," I say. "It's his head."

My father steps toward us and slips his arm under Ernesto's left shoulder. Ernesto's legs go limp as Papi and I carry him like a deadweight to my parents' room. They have a real bed, a wedding present from Mami's side of the family. Carefully, we lift him onto the bed. He lies down, groaning as Papi lifts his legs into place.

I can hear Mami sobbing in the doorway. I turn and find her glaring at me, her face a wet ruin.

"What happened?" she cries.

"Two guys dropped him off. They said he crashed his truck. I didn't know them."

She wipes her tears and approaches the bed. "Ernesto. *Mi hijo.* Can you hear me?"

"*Si,*" he whispers.

"Can you breathe?"

"*Si,* Mami."

"Where do you hurt?"

"My head, Mami."

"Can you move your hands? Your feet?"

"*Si, si.* Mami ... but my head's going to explode."

She strokes Ernesto's damp hair away from his forehead like he's a little boy who's fallen off his bicycle. At first he winces, but then he seems to relax slightly. She starts humming songs from church, songs telling my brother that Jesús loves him, that Jesús forgives him, and that Jesús will care for him.

Papi turns to me.

"Diego," he says. "Go get the doctor."

THERE'S ONLY ONE DOCTOR in Corazón de la Fuente, a guy named Ramirez who's not exactly young. He lives in a little row house opposite the church. By the time I get there I'm out of breath. No lights are on, but I tap on the door. When there's no answer I knock harder and start calling, "Doctor! Doctor!"

I hear shuffling footsteps. The door swings open. Señora Ramirez stands peering up at me, her lined face a question mark.

"It's Diego, *si?*" Her voice is rough with sleep. "Diego Hernandez?"

"*Si, si.* Is your husband here, señora?"

"Where else would he be, muchacho? Is everything all right?"

"No. My brother's been in an accident."

"That new truck of his?"

"*Si,*" I say, and she nods and turns away. I wait on the stoop, shuffling to keep warm. Through the open door, I watch Dr. Ramirez step out of his bedroom. He's small and plump like his wife, with a thick, white mustache he gets trimmed every Saturday morning at the barbershop. It's weird to see him unshaven, his face covered with white stubble. He's wearing a flannel pajama top, which he tucks into the waist of his Levi's.

"Where's my bag?" he says, peering around the dark room. "Irena, have you seen my bag?"

"In the kitchen."

He spots it. It's on a counter near the two-burner stove. He picks it up and barges past me, heading toward the plaza. I follow him, at times breaking into a jog to keep up. It's turned so cold I can see his breath in the air, looking like little puffs of mist. I can't believe how quickly he can move. We pass the old well and move down crooked lanes and then we're at my house.

"Doctor!" my mother cries. "Thank God you've come!" She seizes him by the elbow and leads him to Ernesto, who's still motionless and pale on the bed. His eyes flit from me to the doctor to my parents.

Dr. Ramirez lifts Ernesto's limp hand and feels for a pulse. He nods, and fishes a flashlight out of his bag. He shines it in Ernesto's eyes.

"I'm guessing your head hurts," the doctor says to my brother.

Ernesto winces. The doctor looks at the rest of us. "Please. Let me examine the patient."

We all back out of the room. We sit, not talking, Mami rocking and praying under her breath. After fifteen minutes or so, Dr. Ramirez comes out. Mami and Papi jump to their feet. It all feels like a hospital *telenovela*—people are always getting into car accidents in Mexican soap operas, except that we're in a small town, and the nearest hospital is more than an hour away.

"How is he?" asks Mami.

The doctor shrugs. "I don't think he's got any broken bones, though you'll want to get his collarbone x-rayed at some point. The real question is his head. The boy has a pretty decent concussion—that much is for sure. The left pupil is fine, but the right one's as big as an apple. Ideally, he'd be in the hospital, but when I think of the drive along that bumpy highway to Laredo … ay. My suggestion is you keep him here and watch him. If he starts thinking he's somewhere else, we'll need to get him to the city. If he starts vomiting, or becomes unresponsive, he'll have to go as well, the highway be damned. In the morning, I'll have another look at him and we might take him in anyway, do you understand?"

"We do," says Papi.

"In the meantime, keep an eye on him. It's tonight I'm worried about."

The doctor packs up and leaves. With everything going on, I'm not sure anyone bothered to thank him or pay him. Mami makes coffee and snacks, while Papi steps out the back door and has a smoke.

Which leaves me in the living room, watching the four walls and wondering what might happen next. After a couple of minutes, I can't stand it any longer, so I go outside and join my father.

"You aren't smoking yet?" he asks.

"No."

"You plan to?"

"No."

"Good. Keep it that way. Filthy habit. I nearly quit once, you know?"

"I know."

"But lately … it's a difficult thing."

A coydog brays somewhere far off. The moon's a perfect circle.

"Papi," I say. "Don't worry. Ernesto will be all right."

He releases a blue-gray funnel into the night air. Little bugs, tiny moths and mosquitoes, light up in the smoke.

"The sad truth is, Ernesto hasn't been all right for a while now."

Papi lifts his cigarette to his mouth and takes in another suicidal lungful. Since we saw those dead bodies, it's been like this, Papi telling me things that you'd tell another man and not your boy. I like it, even though it makes me uncomfortable.

"You know who caused all of this, don't you? It was that damn woman of his."

"*Si*," I say. "It was Violeta."

7

THE DOCTOR, as he promised, comes back in the morning. This time, he lets us all crowd into the room when he shines a light into Ernesto's eyes, the patient blinking and pushing him away and mumbling that he wants to sleep. "His signs aren't improving," Ramirez says. "But they aren't getting worse, either. I'll come back this afternoon."

Later, I hear Ernesto puking into the pan next to his bed. Mami leaps up and races into the room. "*Hijo!*" I hear her say. "Are you all right? Do you need the doctor again?"

When Mami comes out, her eyes find me. "His head is killing him, Diego. He can't stand any light and he can't stand noises so we'll have to be quiet, do you understand?"

"*Si*, Mami. I get it."

Dr. Ramirez comes and goes over the next two days. By the end of it, Ernesto seems a little better. He's regained some color, and he can sit up and open his eyes and talk like a normal person so long as the curtains are drawn.

"If his concussion was going to kill him," Ramirez tells my parents, "it would have done so by now. But that boy's got a banged-up head, and he'll be recuperating for a while. My guess is he'll be in that room for a couple of weeks. Maybe even a month or more."

Mami looks relieved. "So he's going to be all right?"

"I believe so. With time. You have God to thank for that."

"*Si*," says Mami while crossing herself. "*Gracias*, doctor. You're right. This was a blessing of God."

AT NIGHT, my parents sleep in the room that Ernesto and I ordinarily sleep in. I've got the sofa, which is as old as the house itself. I'm constantly adjusting myself, tossing and turning so my body's not poked by one of the loosened springs. During the day, Mami busies herself by cooking broth for Ernesto, dabbing his forehead with a damp sponge, and helping him go to the bathroom without getting up. It's like he's some sort of baby, and if I know Mami, there's a small part of her that likes having an infant again, even one the size of Ernesto.

She's getting tired though. Dark pouches have appeared beneath her eyes, and she's constantly muttering to herself. One afternoon, about four days after the accident, Papi stops her in the middle of the kitchen as she's about to warm some chicken *caldo*. He puts his hands on her shoulders.

"Rest, *amor*."

"Eduardo, I can't. There are so many things to be done."

"What things?"

"Shopping, for one. We're out of food."

"I'll do the shopping. You need to rest. You've been awake for days."

"I haven't."

"You *have*. You think I don't hear you praying in the middle of the night?"

"But Ernesto needs—"

"He needs nothing. You just looked in on him. He's sound asleep, Helena."

"What if he wakes up?"

"Diego's here. Look at you. You can barely keep your eyes open. Your fingers are trembling with fatigue."

"Well, then …"

"Well, then, go to bed. Your boy is fine. The doctor said so. Now rest."

Mami mutters something under her breath and goes into the bedroom. Papi comes over and sits down opposite me. The chair creaks. It's missing a leg and we use an old wooden box to prop it up.

"Diego, I'm going to the cantina to have one bottle of Tecate with my friends. I'll do the shopping on the way home. In the meantime, can you keep an eye on that brother of yours?"

WE ONLY GET THREE STATIONS and I keep flipping between them: football, news, soap opera. Football, news, soap opera. Monterrey defeated Oaxaca, three to one. The American president, Barack Obama, is meeting with the Mexican president, Felipe Calderón, to discuss the financial crisis. A beautiful movie star with fake *tetas* is in a hospital bed, having mysteriously lost her vision.

It's the same old garbage, and I wish I had a laptop so I could watch YouTube, assuming I could find Wi-Fi in our dusty little town—the connection seems to come and go with the weather. A long time ago, Corazón was home to the world's most powerful radio tower, or at least it was until the gringo who built it was arrested for not paying taxes and left the thing to fall apart. These days, I have to go to the library and log on to one of their crappy, sticky-key computers just to send an e-mail, and half the time even that doesn't work.

I'm bored. I turn the set off. My mother is snoring lightly in Ernesto's hammock. Then I hear a weak voice, coming from my parents' bedroom: it's Ernesto, calling for me.

I go in.

"What is it?"

He has a hand over his eyes, as if he can't bear even the small amount of light in the room. I figure the sound of my steps probably hurt him too.

"*Hermano*," he whispers. "Close the curtains."

"They already are."

He opens his eyes and squints at me. "Ay," he says. "I was having a dream. Salma Hayek, *primo*. Salmita herself. Imagine ..." He starts to chuckle and then stops suddenly, gasping. He lifts his hand to hold his forehead.

"Sit," he says in a soft voice. "We need to talk."

There's a chair beside the bed and I sit on a little pile of Ernesto's undershirts. That's when I notice something. His eyes are wet.

Ernesto's eyes are red and wet, and beneath the redness you can see the bruising I gave him when we bare-knuckled in the desert. It's blue and green and yellow, and I figure, *Good, serves you right.*

He wipes away a tear. "Diego. I screwed up."

"Yeah. You did."

"It's not the truck."

"It's that thick head of yours. Don't worry, *hermano.* It'll get better."

"I'm not talking about that either."

"What is it then?"

"Ay, Diego. I screwed up this time."

"So you say. If it's not your head or your truck, what're you talking about?"

He opens his eyes and looks at me, blinking away the pain. It's like he's trying to make me understand without having to tell me.

That's when I get it. My skin turns cold.

"It's the Silverado. The Coahuilans fronted you the money, didn't they?"

"Diego … I'm sorry."

"So you'll pay them back."

He rocks his head from one side to the other and then stops, hissing air beneath his teeth. His chest is rising and falling. "No," he says weakly. "No."

"*Hermano.* What're you telling me?"

He covers his face with his hands. He's sobbing now, and can't speak. When I imagine the worst it's suddenly there, like a third person in the room with us, jeering.

"You were going to do a job for the Coahuilans. You were going to earn the money they gave you for the truck."

He sniffles and takes a huge breath. "*Si*," he says, his voice muffled behind his hand.

"What were you going to do?"

"A delivery. In *el norte*."

My heart's pumping. I know there's no easy answer to this problem, but I try to find one anyway.

"So do it later."

"There is no later with them. There's a schedule, Diego, and it has to be met. This is big business we're talking about. I'm already late and in their world late doesn't happen. You know what they'll do to me if the delivery isn't made?"

His eyes fill again. I can see the humiliation hurts him worse than the concussion. I don't care. His head can hurt him all it wants.

What he says next changes everything. "It's not just me."

The third man in the room? He's cackling now, loving every second.

"Ernesto. What do you mean?"

His voice is little more than a whisper. "For what I owe them, it won't just be me, Diego."

My head spins. I picture Mami and Papi, and the worried looks that are always on their faces. I picture the way they've been running around, caring for him, feeding him, cleaning him up, making sure he gets better. I hate Ernesto with everything I have.

I squeeze my eyes shut. I'm trembling all over. There's only one thing to be done.

"Goddamn you to hell."

"Hell would be better than this, Diego."

"I have to do it for you."

"No! You can't."

The idea is like a gale-force wind now that it's been said out loud. "It's either me or Papi and you can't ask Papi."

"No, Diego. You don't know what's involved—"

"So what then?"

"You can't. It's dangerous."

"It's too dangerous not to."

"I can't let you."

"This is no longer up to you, *cabrón*."

I watch him think. His voice sounds garbled, like he's speaking underwater.

"*Hermano*. I'm sorry."

Ernesto motions me toward him. He's pale and shaky. He's worn himself out, and every word is an ordeal.

"In our bedroom …," he whispers.

"*Sí?*"

"In the lower drawer of our dresser … there are some things you'll need."

He's closed his eyes and is holding his head. I back away from the bed and sneak into our bedroom. Mami is still snoring lightly, her mouth open and her hands resting on her belly. I open the drawer slowly so the creak won't wake her.

There's nothing there but Ernesto's jeans and a few T-shirts. I push them aside, and then I see it. It's dark blue and the size of a pack of cigarillos.

A Mexican passport.

8

BACK IN THE LIVING ROOM, I open the passport. The head shot is Ernesto's, though the name on the inside page is "Hector Valdez." Hector is twenty and was born in Saltillo. Tucked into the pages are a few gringo twenty-dollar bills, as well as a laminated driver's license, again in the name of "Hector Valdez," and the photo, again, is of my brother. My face is a beefier version of Ernesto's and with any luck the guard at the gringo border will just think I've gained a little weight since the photo was taken.

Or at least that's my hope.

I find Vincente outside his house, sitting on an old kitchen chair, a Tejano hat keeping the sun out of his eyes. Three or four small children from the neighboring houses play around him.

He takes one look at me and knows something's up.

"Vincente, I need to talk to you."

"Okay, okay. Take it easy."

We walk down his street, reaching a long, jacal-style house that was abandoned long ago. If the rumors are correct, it used to be a whorehouse and was the reason the town was formed in the first place—so horny gringos would have somewhere to go on a Saturday night. Now the locals use it as a place to protect their pigs and mules from bad weather.

Just beyond is the ruined radio tower. We stand directly underneath its base, amid twisted bits of metal and rubber that have fallen from it.

"So," he says. "What's so important?"

"Ernesto borrowed money from the Coahuilan Cartel to buy his truck. He was going to earn the money back but now the stupid *hijo de puta* can't work. He can't even get out of bed without throwing up."

"It's time you told me straight," he says. "What exactly does Ernesto do for them?"

"He delivers packages over the border."

"What's in the packages?"

I don't need to answer. My expression does it for me.

"Ay no," Vincente says.

"If I don't go in his place, they'll kill him. They'll kill Mami and Papi too. Maybe me as well."

"So you have to do it."

"Soon as possible. He's already late, the stupid *pendejo*."

"I'd do it too."

I feel a little better, even though nothing has changed.

"Diego," he says. "Take a walk with me."

Vincente turns and marches back in the direction of his house. We stop at a little hovel just three doors down from his place. There are red velvet curtains over the window and a star within a circle drawn on the door.

I've heard of this woman.

"Listen," says Vincente. "Whenever people need some luck, they come here."

"You've got to be kidding."

"I'm not. You remember when my *abuela* needed to get her gallbladder taken out? She came here before the operation and everything turned out fine. And remember the time my aunt had that tumor inside her? She came here and she got better."

"I don't believe in this stuff."

"You don't have to. As long as the *curandera* does."

Vincente knocks. A wizened old woman with chin hairs answers. I'm hit with a strange odor, like roasting corn mixed with chicken shit.

"Vincente Oroyo," the old woman croaks. One of her eyes is filmy and blue.

"*Si*, señora."

"And his good friend Diego Hernandez."

"*Si*," I say, surprised she knows my name.

"Why are you muchachos here?"

"It's Diego," says Vincente. "He has to do something dangerous."

"What's that?"

"We can't tell you."

She chuckles. Her eyes shine with knowing, even though the right one is all messed up.

"Does it have to do with that brother of his? The one named Ernesto?"

"Please, señora. We can't say."

"It doesn't matter. Danger is danger. It's all the same. It's like water or air." She's peering at us. Her head is turned slightly to favor her good eye. "Well, if you're coming in, now would be a good time."

We enter her little house. There are old newspapers everywhere. A cat is sleeping in the corner. My eyes keep landing on random items. A dented pot sitting on the floor. A theater magazine turned yellow with age. A single slipper with a hole in the toe.

The old woman rummages through a pantry filled with jars and flasks. She pulls one down and sniffs it. She comes over.

"Sit," she says to me.

"Please, señora. Really, I—"

"*Sit*," she says again, and to humor her I lower myself onto an old kitchen chair. She stays standing. She's so small we're eye to eye.

She unscrews the jar and dips her fingers into a white powder. She smears some of the powder on my forehead.

"There," she says.

"What is it?"

"Cascarilla eggshell powder. It'll help protect you. It's an old Santeria trick."

I glance over at Vincente.

"*Gracias*, señora, but I have to—"

"You have to what? Be someplace? I know that, muchacho. That's why you're here. You have to go someplace you don't want to go. The powder will help, but only a little. What'll really help is you. If you go just because you *have* to, you will not succeed. If you go with resentment and bitterness in your heart, you will be defeated. But if you go with a pure heart … if you go with a goal in mind, if you go because you want to *achieve* something, the saints will look fondly upon you. So you ask yourself, Diego Hernandez: What is it you want out of your mission?"

She's crazy, I think.

"Señora," I tell her. "Really, I have to go."

"So who's keeping you? Look at the size of you, muchacho. You think I could stop a bruiser like you? That'll be ten pesos, by the way."

I put a coin in her outstretched palm. She trundles toward the back of her house, muttering to herself.

In the street, I look at Vincente as I wipe the powder off my face.

"I know," he says. "I know. It's a little strange. I just thought …" His voice trails off. "When do you go, Diego?"

"In the morning."

We both feel awkward.

"Good luck, *nini*," he says, and then he turns and walks away.

THAT NIGHT I LIE AWAKE on our moth-eaten sofa, struggling to sleep. I finally drift off, only to be awakened by the pale dawn light filtering through the window. My head pounds and my mouth is dry.

I get up before Mami and have a glass of warm Milo. Papi is already awake and in his armchair.

"Papi," I say. "Ernesto's asked me to pick up some of his things in Laredo."

"How are you getting there?"

"I thought maybe you could lend me the Datsun."

Papi lowers his paper. It's like he's inspecting me, though after a few seconds he lifts up his paper again.

They Found His Severed Body Parts in the Sewer! says the headline.

"Be careful," I hear from behind the paper. "You know I took your mother on our first date in this car …"

I go to see Ernesto. He's still lying in my parents' bed, eyes open, listening. I sit next to him.

"You knew I'd do it," I say.

"Diego, I—"

"All of your protests, saying how you won't let me, how dangerous it is. All of it was acting."

"Diego, I swear—"

"Don't worry, *hermano*. I'm still going. I just want you to understand that I know. I want you to understand you're stupider than me and you can't fool me."

He lowers his head back on the pillow and exhales. Normally he'd attack me for saying something like that. If I'm getting my revenge, it's by making him lie there and take it. For a few seconds, we say nothing. Then he takes my revenge away from me by saying, in the weakest of voices, "You're right. I am stupid."

Goddamn you, I think.

"Get me a pen and paper," he says.

I go into the kitchen and rummage around. When I give him the paper he writes down an address in Nuevo Laredo.

"You're going to see a man, Diego."

"What's his name?"

He pauses. He licks his dry lips and says nothing.

"Out with it," I tell him.

"Everyone calls him El Tranquilo."

I swallow hard. It's a name I know. It's a name everyone knows. "Tell me you're joking."

"He's not as bad as people say. Most of those things—they're tales told by old women."

I'm forcing myself to breathe. "Did he leave those bodies out on the highway?"

"I don't know."

"Yes, Ernesto. Yes you do."

Ernesto closes his eyes slowly. "Diego ... this address ... it's out by the old fairgrounds. You remember the old fairgrounds? Where we went as kids?" He winces, as if the memory hurts him. "Later, when you get to the border, tell the customs agent you're going to visit your aunt. Tell them she's sick and needs help. It's the story I always use. And after you get through, don't start smiling. They catch a lot of people that way. They look happy once they're through so the guards know something's up. Just look like you've crossed a thousand times. Just act like you're bored."

"All right."

"You'll be fine."

"All right."

"I know you will. You can do this."

I leave the house and get in Papi's car. For a moment I sit and listen—a village like ours makes its own sounds when it starts to come alive in the mornings, roosters cawing and pigs rooting and babies crying. Many of our neighbors have their kitchens outside, sticking out of the backs of their houses, kept dry under an awning fashioned from old vegetable stakes. I can smell the smoke of a dozen breakfast fires, all smoldering under pots of water. All the times I've dreamt of leaving Corazón and suddenly I don't want to leave. I don't want to go to a place where that smell doesn't greet me at every turn.

I turn the key, pumping the accelerator exactly three times. The starter whirrs and whirrs and whirrs.

Finally, the motor comes alive in a cloud of blue-gray smoke.

9

▽△▽△▽△▽

I DRIVE SLOWLY out of the village. The road connecting the town to the highway is cracked and potholed, and I'm worried the suspension might break if I go too fast. The sun is still low in the sky, and everything's cast in a pale orange glow.

Once I reach the highway, I hit the accelerator, the car rattling as I get close to the speed limit. The engine is whining loudly, and my hands jiggle against the steering wheel. It's like this for the next half hour, the Datsun shaking madly as I drive through the desert. All I can do is hope the engine doesn't overheat or something doesn't break and fall off the bottom of the car. I'm probably the only driver on the road who's thankful when the traffic slows on the way into Nuevo Laredo.

Off in the distance I see the spine of Nuevo's rickety old roller coaster. The Red Devil, it was called. I drive toward it, thinking of the times Papi took us to the fairground when it was open in the summer. That was before everything changed, when Mexico still had its own carnivals and people didn't just cross the border and go to one of the Six Flags in Texas or Arizona.

I remember clowns and games of skill and the lunches Mami used to pack, *tacos el pastor* with huge chunks of mild creamy cheese and cans of Coca-Cola she'd keep cold by wrapping them in newspaper. But the main attraction was the Red Devil, the biggest roller coaster in all of northern Mexico. We didn't care that the fairgrounds in Juárez and Saltillo and Monterrey all made the same claim about *their* roller coasters; that first ascent still seemed to go on forever, *clack clack clack clack clack* and all you could do was grip the bar while you looked up at an endless wash of blue, until finally you'd come over the crest and you'd scream like death itself was chasing you.

There was this one time, though. We were chugging toward the first drop and Ernesto turned to me and said, "At the top I'm going to do something."

"What?"

"Never you mind. You just do it too."

I didn't say no and I didn't say yes, though I had a feeling I wouldn't like it. I was seven or eight and he was nine or ten. The car kept climbing and I wasn't thinking about the height or the drop or Mami and Papi, far down below, little specks with hands shielding their eyes. I was worrying about what my brother was going to do.

Just before we reached the top, Ernesto took off his seat belt, which was little more than a frayed band and a cheap plastic buckle. "Come on!" he howled at me, and while I stayed pinned to my seat my crazy brother stood straight up, throwing his hands in the air and howling, waiting until the exact moment the car crested the hill before sitting back down. Then we plunged. At

the end of the ride, we stepped out of our car onto a little platform, Ernesto still laughing and me feeling like I was the one
who was about to get in trouble. "Don't do that again," said the
ride's operator, an old campesino with gold teeth and a cowboy
hat. "You do that again and you're banned."

We stepped through the exit turnstile. Papi charged up, red in
the face. "You think that was funny?" he spat at Ernesto.

"Chill, Papacito, it's—"

And that's when Papi slapped Ernesto across the face. He
didn't do it hard, but the point is he did it. I looked over at Mami,
who was too shocked to say a thing. Ernesto just stood there, a
hand on his cheek, eyes welling. "Don't you ever use that tone
with me," said Papi. "I'll take us all home right now." He turned
to me. "Diego, you hear that? I'm talking to you too."

Though we didn't go home, the day was ruined. Yes, we went in
the haunted house and we rode the bumper cars and we watched
the evening rodeo and we ate the food Mami had packed. But it
wasn't the same. It was like some happiness had been sucked out
of the day.

That night, as soon as Ernesto got me alone in our bedroom,
he caught me in a vicious headlock.

"Why didn't you stand up? Why not? It's cause you're chickenshit, isn't it? Say it! Say you're chickenshit!"

I couldn't breathe. I was little and terrified and I thought he
might actually kill me. "I'm chickenshit!" I croaked.

"Again!"

"I'm chickenshit!"

"All right, then."

He let me go and I stood there trying not to cry. But he was wrong. I wasn't afraid to stand up. I wasn't afraid of flying out of the car or of making Papi mad. The truth was, I just didn't want the attention. I didn't like the idea of everyone down below pointing up and yelling, *Look at that crazy* niño!

But not Ernesto. For him, that was the reason he did it.

I DRIVE AROUND and for the millionth time I wish I had a smart phone instead of my crappy old Nokia with the flip-cover. When I find the place, I'm sure I'm at the wrong address: it's a regular cinder-block house, surrounded by mesh wire fencing like so many of the houses in Nuevo Laredo. Since it's out by the old fairgrounds, it's surrounded by empty lots covered in bits of metal and papers. I check the address once more and get out.

There's a buzzer on the fence encircling the house. I press it.

The door of the house opens and a guy comes out. He's the size of a small hill, and he's wearing a three-piece suit he must have had specially made. His hair is in a ponytail and I can see tattoos on his hands and high on his neck.

He walks up to me.

"*Qué*?" he asks in a sandpaper voice.

"I've got an appointment."

He looks at me, up and down. "You got the wrong address. Now get lost."

He's turning back toward the house when I pipe up. "I'm Diego Hernandez. Ernesto Hernandez is my brother."

He stops. His back is as wide as a billboard. He turns and steps back toward to the fence. "Ernesto is your brother?"

"*Si*." I'm out of breath, even though I haven't been running.

"Wait here."

He walks back into the house. I'm left standing at the gate. The sun is beating down on the top of my head. I hear a rooster crow and a car backfire. The door to the house opens again, and the huge man comes toward me. He punches a number into a keypad mounted on his side of the fence, and when the gate door pops open he motions me forward.

"Spread your arms."

His meaty hands run all over my body, even between my legs. When he's finished, he turns and starts walking back toward the house.

After a few steps, the metal gate closes automatically behind me. The giant man enters the house and I follow him inside. It's a middle-class house. There are no hammocks, but then again the furniture looks faded, like it's been around awhile. There's an indoor kitchen with a stove and fridge, though they look like they've seen better days too. If *la nota roja* are correct, this is one of a dozen houses El Tranquilo uses, moving from one to the other whenever he feels unsafe. A few of them, I've heard, are even connected by tunnels.

"Sit," the big man says.

I sit on a cloth-covered sofa whose armrests are worn bare. The big man sits in a chair opposite me, his eyes boring into my chest. There's a coffee table separating us, with magazines spread out. Most of them are American publications, *People* and *Time* and *Reader's Digest*, though there are some Mexican magazines mixed in as well, like *Us En Español*. Running along the wall behind the big man is a painting of the Last Supper, Jesús looking resplendent and calm, Judas off at one end, looking cheerful and sneaky.

My heart.

Hijo de puta, it's pounding.

We wait. The huge man doesn't move except to check his BlackBerry every time it beeps. Finally, a door to another part of the house opens and a man comes out. He's short and stocky, with slightly bowed legs. He's wearing a Miami Dolphins jersey with oily pants and a threadbare ball cap. He's smiling. In fact, he looks as though he can do nothing *but* smile; it's like his face has been molded into a single, mirthful expression.

That's when I realize he's had plastic surgery. I've read about it in *la nota roja*, how it's a common way for cartel bosses to avoid detection. Sure enough, when El Tranquilo speaks, his lips barely move. It's like he's a ventriloquist, minus the dummy. The skin of his face looks as if it's made from putty and not actual flesh. His teeth are as white as a rabbit's fur, and I'd bet they're false as well.

"I see you've met Ramón," he says in a voice so quiet I have to strain to hear it. There's a third chair in the room, positioned next to the one filled by Ramón. El Tranquilo sits. "I hear you've come in your brother's place."

"*Sí.*"

"And your name's Diego?"

I nod.

"Let me tell you something, Diego. I know your brother. He's an idiot, but at least I know him. But you … you I don't know. I got no idea whether I can trust you and this bothers me."

"I—"

"Let me finish, *cabrón*. Your brother owes me money, which he can't repay because he crashed his new truck and banged up his head. So he sends you in his place, only I don't trust you. Your *brother*, Diego, has put me in this situation, you got me?"

I can tell he's furious but still there's that waxy semi-grin, like something painted on a mannequin's face.

"So I'm gonna ask you a question, and you better think before answering. If you were me, what would you do?"

"I'd trust me."

"Why?"

"I saw those bodies on the highway."

He takes a deep breath. It's like he's studying me, like he's looking for a sign of some sort. After a few seconds, he turns to his henchman and nods. The big man rises and leaves the room. As we wait, I notice little things. Tranquilo's eyes are a steely gray. His fingernails are nicely trimmed. Along with his crappy clothes and torn ball cap he's wearing a brand-new gold Rolex.

Ramón comes back into the room, the floor groaning beneath his bulk. He's carrying a small leather bag that reminds me of the one Dr. Ramirez toted when he treated Ernesto. He places it carefully on the glass coffee table in front of me. After unzipping the bag, he pulls out four bricks, each wrapped in white paper. They're all stamped with a pair of linked *C*s.

"Look," says Tranquilo. "That's four kilos of uncut black tar heroin. You know what that is?"

"I think so."

"No you don't. I can tell just by lookin' at you." He leans forward, hands on his knees, and sighs, like he's resentful he has to explain. "We grow the poppies here in this country, in Sinaloa. Asian heroin is white and powdery, ours is black and sludgy, like tar. We make it that way on purpose. This way, no one's ever gonna confuse the two. You following me, *joven*?"

I nod. My throat feels constricted, and I'm not sure I could speak even if I wanted to.

"The DEA just found one of my tunnels, those *hijos de putas*. So now I got a problem, *si*? Until we build another tunnel, I've got to increase the number of shipments made over the border, instead of under it. This is where people like your brother come in, only most of them are smart enough to stay out of traffic accidents. So now I'm forced to trust you, someone I don't know, and I'm a man who doesn't like being forced into things."

He waits a few seconds, and then hands me a piece of paper.

"This is the address of a guy in San Antonio. His name is Crazy J. Can't say you're going to like meeting him."

Tranquilo puts the bricks back into the bag and walks toward the door. For some reason, I look at Ramón, who nods. I stand up and follow Tranquilo, the big man trailing behind us. When we reach the gate, Tranquilo spots the car I've driven in.

"You're using that car?"

I take a deep breath. It's over, I think. He won't let me do this in Papi's ancient Datsun.

"*Si*," I admit.

"Smart. Has it been fixed?"

I don't understand the question, so I shake my head no.

"Go around the corner. The place is called Saturn 400 Auto Body. They'll make it right. I'll let them know you're coming."

"*Si, gracias*."

His eyes narrow as he looks me up and down. It's like he's adding figures, or trying to solve a riddle. "You're different than your brother, that right, *hijo*?"

"*Sí.*"

"Good."

He opens the gate and hands me the bag. I step through and hear the gate shut behind me.

"Diego?"

I turn to look back at El Tranquilo. His too-white teeth glisten in the sun.

"I got enough problems," he says. "Don't give me another."

10

▲▽▲▽▲▽

THE YARD IN FRONT OF SATURN 400 is littered with old wrecks and spare tires. A few mechanics are leaning into the hoods of Volkswagen Beetles, rusting Oldsmobiles, and battered Ford F-150s, though they all stop and look at me when I pull up to the curb. Behind them is a garage with three bays, two of them filled with cars. Attached to the garage is a small office. There's no sign, but I know I'm in the right spot.

A muscular guy with a hairnet comes out. He's wearing a shiny blue buttoned shirt, his forearms green with tattoos. The toothpick between his teeth dances when he talks.

"You Ernesto's brother?

"Yeah."

"You look like him."

"People say that."

"Bigger, though."

He takes a step back and studies the Datsun, one eyebrow lifting. "Damn, *cabrón*. That is one ugly ride. I'm surprised you even made it here. Now do me a favor and drive it into the garage. That is, if the thing'll move."

He laughs as I put the Datsun in gear. Once I shut off the engine, he presses a red plastic button that lowers a corrugated tin door, hiding the car from view. I step out. The place smells of oil and sweat.

"So, muchacho. Where's the package?"

I freeze.

"Relax, muchacho. Where is it?"

"It's in the trunk."

"The spare-tire compartment, by any chance? Good idea. The cops'd never think of looking *there*." He laughs again. "Don't worry, *primo*. Your secret's safe with me. We'll get you done up right. Now wait in the office and don't break anything."

THERE ARE A FEW NEWSPAPERS and some gringo car magazines on a small table. I pick up an issue of *Road & Track* and start thumbing through it. It's full of ultra-expensive sports cars. A month ago, I'd have drooled over all those Porsches and Ferraris, wishing one of them was mine. But now I look at them and wonder how many of us will ruin our lives to get one. And not just by doing crimes, like Ernesto. My head spins, imagining the number of dumb-ass muchachos who stick with jobs they can't stand, or suck up to bosses they hate, just so they can get paid enough to make the monthly payment on a Viper.

I put the magazine down. My hands are trembling and I feel weak. I realize I haven't eaten since morning, and even then it was just a glass of instant breakfast. I walk out onto the street and buy a plate of tacos from a roadside vendor. I go back inside. Norteño music is playing from a tinny radio. I listen for a bit, trying to place the song. I know I know it from somewhere, and then it hits me that they played it at that party I went to with Vincente and Fernando, the one where Rosita kissed me under the desert moonlight and I felt nothing. Funny how long ago that seems.

Even though I can guess what Mami and Papi and Ernesto are doing right now, I wish I knew for sure. I want to know that Papi is reading his newspaper, glowering all the while. I want to know that Mami is making *caldo* for Ernesto, and that Ernesto is lying in their bedroom, guarding his eyes, since in Mexico at midday it's impossible to fully darken a room. Then, I picture the features of my town, Corazón de la Fuente. I picture the church with no spire and the rusting old radio tower. I picture the long, low building where women used to sell their bodies. I picture the old graveyard, where the revolutionary leader's grandniece lies buried in her tiny coffin. I picture the mission, overlooking the town, as if guarding it from banditos. I picture the old well, and I wonder whether Mami has already hung her head inside it and sadly told the specters in its depths about Ernesto and his banged-up head.

Two hours later, the guy with the hairnet comes and gets me. "All right, gangster. It's ready to go."

He leads me to the car and opens the passenger-side door. Then he pops the glove box and pulls out the maps and cigarettes Papi keeps in there.

"You see it?"

"See what?"

"Look closer, *cabrón*. Look closer."

I peer into the gloom of the glove box.

"I don't see anything."

"Look closer."

I lean in tighter and that's when I see it. A small panel has been installed.

"You see it now?"

"*Si*."

"Open it."

I reach in and try to dislodge the panel, though without anything to hold on to it's not easy. I try pushing it but that doesn't work either. "It won't budge," I tell him.

"Now watch."

He climbs in the driver's side. "You have to do two things, and you have to do them in the right order. Number one. Turn on the car's electrical system, but do *not* turn the motor on. You understand me?" He half-turns the key. The dashboard lights weakly flicker and the radio comes on, some old-timer's station Papi likes, the announcer speaking in a jumble of English and Spanish. The mechanic makes a face and turns the radio off. "Number two. Engage the parking brake. If the parking brake already *was* on, you'll have to start all over."

He pulls up the brake lever and I hear a muffled *pop*.

"Look," he says.

The face of the panel has fallen into the glove box, revealing a hold about the size of a shoe box. The drugs are in there, the four bricks the exact size of the hiding spot.

"It's all lined with asbestos. The dogs shouldn't smell a thing."

"What about the leather bag?"

"Don't you worry about that. And as for paying me, the boss says it's on your account, you got that?"

"*Si*."

The door to the garage is still closed so I can't get in and drive away.

"I'm thinking," says the mechanic, "you've never done this before."

"No."

"Don't worry. It isn't hard. To get it done you just need one thing."

I take a breath. "What's that?"

"*Huevos* the size of baseballs!" He laughs loudly and slams his hand against the red plastic button. The garage door grinds open.

"Good luck!" he calls as I back the car out. "And remember … baseballs, *hijo*, baseballs!"

I DRIVE THROUGH A DESOLATE AREA with nothing but auto shops and vacant lots. After a few minutes, I start passing cinder-block homes with entire families sitting outside to avoid the baking heat indoors. After a bit, I near the center of town and spot the huge white customs and immigration building that marks the border with Texas. I drive toward it, only to get turned around in a warren of streets near the market, so I unroll the window and call for directions from an old woman selling woven dolls and wispy straw hats.

She points a shaky hand, and I drive in that direction. Once I clear the market buildings, I can see I'm close, just a few more turns and then I'm at the border. There are two lanes. The first is for gringos leaving Mexico, and it's empty. The second is for Mexicans entering *el norte*, and it stretches for close to a mile.

I pull in to that line, the Datsun backfiring as it settles into an uneven idle. Even with my window open, there's no air, just thick, humid vapor. Vendors walk up and down the line of cars, selling bottles of water, candy, tamales, and newspapers. One leans his head in my window, startling me.

"Coca-Cola, amigo?" He grins, his mouth full of tin. "You might be here awhile. A muchacho can get thirsty ..."

I buy a can and sip it, my heart racing.

Don't think, I tell myself.

Don't think.

THE LINE IS MOVING SO, SO SLOWLY. Most of the time it's completely still. I move ahead one car, and then stop for five minutes, the Datsun stalling so often I get sick of the sound of the starter motor, grinding away every time I have to start the damn engine. I move ahead one car, stop for five minutes. My head begins to ache and my stomach starts to churn and I worry I might need to find a baño. I inch forward, stop, inch forward, stop. I think about buying a burrito from one of the vendors and leaving it on the seat beside me. That way, if there *are* dogs, the scent of the food might throw them off. On the other hand, it could attract them to the spot where the package is hidden, and isn't it illegal to carry food over the border anyway?

I decide against it. The Coca-Cola tastes weird, like the syrup has gone off. There are no cup holders in Papi's ancient car, so I have to hold the can. I can feel it growing warm in my hand. Flies buzz around the opening, trying to drink the sugary fluid, and the sight of them starts to make me uncomfortable, like they're a bad sign.

Steady, *cabrón*.

Steady.

The dogs *shouldn't* smell a thing.

I MOVE FORWARD another car length and stop. The radio's so old you have to turn a dial to adjust the stations, though any music I find jangles my nerves so I turn it off and listen to the noises coming from the long, long tarmac. There are vendors calling out and music playing from other cars and every once in a while a voice comes over a loudspeaker, telling everyone to please have their passports ready. Off in the distance is a little church, next to the big white building, with a cross mounted on its peaked roof. I can't help it, I cross myself.

One car length forward.

Wait.

One car length forward.

Wait.

My mind's spinning. When I was eight or maybe nine, my parents decided to take us to visit one of my mother's eight sisters, the one who married a Texan who did drywalling in a place called Crystal City. The weather was hot and I'd eaten a bunch of chili candy and *chupa chups* on the way. When we finally got to the front of the line, the friendliest man in the world started talking to us in English. He had a bald head and funny gold glasses and the biggest smile I'd ever seen. He asked to see our passports and when Papi handed them over he started looking through them. First, he took Papi's and held it up, comparing the picture to Papi himself. "Well, that's you all right!" he said as he opened another of our passports, and with the way he kept glancing at Mami I knew it was hers. Meanwhile he was chattering away, "You know I've always wanted to go to Mexico. You think I'd have gone already, given what I do all day, but I've just never really found the time … I hear the food y'all got down there can't be beat."

He handed Mami back her passport.

"I'm afraid y'all are going to have to leave the line."

"What?" said Papi.

"Your wife's passport. It expires in two months."

"We're only going for three days."

"Could be y'all decide to stay awhile, and we can't have undocumented visitors in the United States of America, now can we?"

"But it won't expire!"

"Sir," the man said, his face suddenly changing. "Is there a problem here?"

So we drove back to Corazón. I'd never seen Papi so red in the face. He kept hammering the steering wheel, and saying, "Those *idiotas*, those *pendejos*, those *hijos de putas*, you think they'd have put a family of gringos through all that? Ay, Helena, if I'd had a pistol back there …"

I'M NOW CLOSE ENOUGH that I can see a guard leaning into the cab of the truck way up at the front of our line. He looks friendly but of course it's all an act.

Another car length. Wait. Another car length. I can't help it, I wonder how Papi would react if the same thing happened to him today. I try to picture him getting mad and striking the steering wheel and swearing like Tony Soprano, but I can't do it, it's like picturing a fish taking a walk. Now that he's lost his job and control of his own home, I can't even imagine Papi having enough energy to *try* to cross the border.

Another car.

Wait.

I need air. I open my window, again. The Coke can is still buzzing with flies. A vendor selling copies of a *nota roja* passes by my open window, yelling, "See the gruesome way he died! See the gruesome way he died!"

I rub my eyes so hard I see angry red slashes in the darkness.

Another car length forward.

Wait.

Another car length forward.

Wait.

I'm about ten cars back when I notice that the customs guards seem to be taking their time with a spindly old campesino in a truck that belches black smoke. The old man's out of his vehicle, gesturing with ancient bronzed hands while a pair of guards start pulling off a bunch of battered chairs he has roped onto the back. Soon, they're even cutting into the seat cushions with blades normally used for opening boxes. The old man pleads with them—even this far away I can hear him yelling, "No, no, *soy inocente*, I no doing nothing!"

Don't think.

Don't think, don't think, don't think.

The old man is still pleading and the border guard crosses his thick arms over his belly, saying nothing, his forearms moving up and down with the rise of his fat gut. Meanwhile the old man is getting more and more frantic, using his crooked little hands to say he's done nothing, he's done nothing, *yo no hice nada.*

I'm sweating all over. My chest is tight and no matter how much air I suck in it doesn't feel like enough.

You can do this, *cabrón*.

You *have* to do this.

The border guard who's been listening to the pleading old man raises his right hand and snaps his fingers. Seconds later, I hear barking. A third guard comes out with a dog on a leash, and the dog is going crazy, yapping and barking and howling and straining at his collar. It isn't a German shepherd or a Doberman or any of those dogs you see on badass cop shows. It's just a skinny, off-brown mutt going berserk, *bark bark bark bark bark*, and they let it jump up on the back of the truck where it sticks its nose in some torn burlap tarps and now it's really losing its mind, jumping and tearing at the tarps and if I had to guess I'd say the old man has something sewn into the seams.

One of the guards steps into the truck and drives it off to one side. Two other guards appear and lead the old man away, beefy hands clutching each of his forearms while the viejo yells, "Those no mine! Those no belonging to me!"

Another car length.

Another car length.

The dog is still there.

The guard leans in my window.

"Passport and driver's license, please."

I pass them over.

I don't smile, and I don't look away. I try to look like someone who's done this a thousand times before.

The dog, circling the car.

Yap yap yap yap yap.

"What's the purpose of your visit, son?"

"I am going to visit my *tia* … er, my *aunt*, in San Antonio."

"Are you carrying any food, weapons, or illegal drugs today?"

"No sir."

He returns to my passport, flipping through the pages, staring at Ernesto's picture, and still the dog is going *yap yap yap yap yap.* He coughs and says, "This your first visit to your *tia?*"

"No sir." The dog has shut up. In my mirror I can see him sniffing around my rear tire and I realize someone's spilled some nachos or something there.

"What part of the city is she in, son?"

"The west part, sir." It's the first thing that comes to me, though I know nothing about San Antonio or Texas or the land of *el norte*, and I curse myself for being so stupid, for not even thinking of rehearsing a lie.

"You mean near that huge shopping plaza with the go-karts?"

I come so, so close to agreeing, for it seems that's what he wants, he wants me to say, *Why, yes sir, we go there all the time,* though for some reason I pause. It's a sixth sense I didn't know I had, choosing that moment to reveal itself.

"I am sorry, sir. I do not know it. Maybe it relocated?"

He nods, hands back the passport and driver's license.

"Have a good trip."

As I drive into Los Estados I remember Ernesto's warning, that I shouldn't smile or look happy for there are people out there, customs people with binoculars, watching. So mostly, I try to look tired and glum, which is easy since it's suddenly the way I feel.

11

⫸⫷⫸⫷⫸

I CATCH A HIGHWAY heading north. It doesn't take me long to realize I might as well still be in Mexico. There's the same mesquite, prickly pear, and huisache trees stretching as far as the eye can see. There are the same vultures drifting in the sky, looking for dead animals. I catch glimpses of deer, bounding over scrubland, and I wonder if people hunt them on this side of the border too. When I turn on the radio, I hear the same stations, playing a garble of English, Spanish, and accordion music.

An hour past the border I stop in a place called Dilley, Texas. It's no more than the intersection of a main street and a railway line, along with a few battered homes showing American flags in the windows. On the north side of the main road is a gas station with a store. Its window looks streaky, like someone started washing it and quit halfway through.

I pull into the station and make sure I lock the Datsun before walking into the shop. It's empty except for the cashier, a young Mexican woman wearing thick eye makeup. She has a tattoo on her hand—a dove in flight—and she's reading the Spanish version of one of those trashy gringo gossip magazines. I can see it's open to a full-page photo of Reese Witherspoon walking a dog in Manhattan. Reese is wearing a ball cap and sunglasses and you'd barely know it was her.

"*Baño?*" I ask the girl.

She looks up, though only for a second, and in that second she reminds me of someone though I can't think of who. She looks back down at her magazine. "That depends," she says with a yawn.

"On what?"

"On whether or not you buyin' something, muchacho."

"All right. I'll have a beef stick and a Coke."

She yawns again and hands me the stuff, which I buy with some of the money Ernesto gave me. Then she hands me a key attached to one of those big plastic spoons you use to lift spaghetti from boiling water. "It's out back," she says.

I walk around the side of the building, past a rusted oil tank and a mongrel tied to a peg. It starts barking and takes a run at me, a rusting chain holding it back. I throw the dog the jerky and walk past a laundry line hung with kids' shirts and socks and underpants swaying in the hot breeze. I can hear a TV playing, and it occurs to me there's a family living in the back of this lonely building. They're watching some American game show, the type Papi says is for idiots but watches anyway.

The door to the *baño* is wedged half-open, and I wonder why the cashier even bothered with the key. Inside, the room smells of piss and mold and strong detergent. The sink is caked with dirt, as is the bar of soap next to the faucet. I fumble for a light and look at myself in the soap-splattered mirror. My hair needs washing and there are dark-gray pouches under my eyes. I lean close. The whites of my eyes are run through with small red veins. As I splash cold water on my face, I can hear the sound made by the family's TV leaking through the walls.

"And now for the next contestant on … *The Price Is Right!*"

There's muffled cheering and applause. With the cold water on my face I feel a little more alert though not exactly better. I shoulder my way back through the door and flip open my phone. It's tough to get a signal so I climb up the side of an old oil tanker that's just beyond the laundry line. I try again, the wind ruffling my T-shirt, and that's when I notice my hands are shaking.

"*Hola?*"

"It's me, Mami."

"Diego?"

"*Si.*"

"Do you have Ernesto's things?"

"Not yet."

"I think he's doing a little better today."

"Good."

"I made him a nice *caldo* and he ate every drop of it. Make sure you get everything he needs."

"Can I speak with Papi?"

I wait a few seconds and then he comes on the line. His voice sounds ragged, like he hasn't used it yet today.

"Diego. Is the Datsun behaving?"

"It's fine, Papi."

"It's running well?"

"Like a dream."

"And they say miracles never happen. Why are you phoning, *hijo*?"

"It's just … I wanted to say I might be spending the night. I don't know yet, but I might look at the college here, see if it interests me."

Papi is quiet. He probably knows I'm lying. There's something between us that lets us read each other's mind, even when we're not in the same room. It's like that with some people.

"All right," he says. "I suppose that's all right."

"*Gracias*, Papi."

"Be careful, *hijo*."

"I will," I say. I hear a crackly version of my own voice echo back to me and then the call goes dead. I walk to the Datsun and start it, exhaust mixing with dust. For a few seconds I can't see six feet in front of me. When the exhaust thins I notice the sullen cashier walking toward me. She lights a cigarette, exhaling funnels of smoke.

She comes up and leans in the window. "You forgetting something, amigo?" she says, pointing to the bathroom key, which I'd put down on the passenger seat.

"Oh right," I say, and I hand it to her, expecting her to roll her eyes and move off. Instead, she keeps leaning on the door frame. Her smoke drifts into my face, and if she cares she doesn't show it.

"Can I ask you something?"

"All right."

"What are you doing out here? Nobody comes around here, ever. Especially people with Mexican license plates."

"I'm on my way to my aunt's house."

"So your aunt lives around here, does she?"

"In San Antonio."

"What's your name?"

"Hector."

"My name's Karina. Why'd you just do that?"

"What?"

"Make up a name. Why would you do that?"

"I didn't."

She shrugs. I keep thinking she'll move off but she doesn't, she just keeps leaning on the open window, smoking and peering at me. It's like the package hidden behind the glove compartment is sending signals, signals she's picking up with invisible antennae.

"Well, Hector. One of your taillights is burned out." She flips her hair out of her face. "And I've got something else to tell you. The interstate is crawling with police and the immigration department. If you don't want to get pulled over by *la migra*, you might want to switch to a local road."

I get out of Papi's Datsun. Sure enough, one of the taillights has gone out; it's like the car is winking. I wonder if it was that way at the border and I was just lucky they didn't notice. The girl takes another deep drag on her cigarette and blows it up into the sky. Her left arm is crossed over her belly, her hip thrust to one side. She has gold streaks in her hair and one of her teeth is capped and I swear I know her from somewhere.

"*Gracias*," I tell her.

"Don't mention it."

She tilts her head and my skin feels warm. It's a power that some señoritas have. When they take notice of you it's like you've won some sort of prize.

"You coming back this way?"

"Maybe."

She nods and looks far off, her eyes narrowing, her foot tapping the pavement.

"Have a nice trip, Hector."

She turns and walks back to the little store. I watch her every step as I get back in the car. In fact, I couldn't look away if I tried.

12

▲▽▲▽▲▽

I TAKE A COUNTRY ROAD that heads more or less in the same direction as the interstate. Every ten kilometers I pass through another dirty town, the houses small and shabby with peeling paint and broken windows and laundry hanging in the yards. I keep seeing cars up on blocks, parked on crabgrass lawns.

I keep driving. There are no sidewalks, and that makes these towns look strange. In Corazón, there are always people out walking, particularly after dinner when the evening is cool and everyone wants to say hello to everyone. Here, the streets are deserted, with people clinging to their porches or sitting in tattered lawn chairs in their front yards, watching. The few gringos I see pass in nice trucks or cars. Everyone else looks like me. The only difference is the Mexicans on this side of the border all have a look in their eyes: a look like some trick has been played on them.

It comes to me with a jolt: the cashier reminded me of Ernesto's old girlfriend. Though the cashier and Violeta didn't look that much alike, they both had slender faces and long straight hair and a hard way about them, like the resentment they felt for the world gave them some sort of power. Suddenly, it's like I'm looking at two things. There's the road in front of me and on top of that, like a gauzy screen, is an image of Violeta, sitting on the sofa with Ernesto, her eyelashes thick with mascara, her hair run through with dark red streaks. She was wearing a Megadeth T-shirt and tight jeans and platform sandals. As soon as Ernesto spotted me, he jumped off the sofa and started patting down his clothes.

Meanwhile, she just sat there, looking up at me, grinning.

"What're you doing home?" asked Ernesto. "It's only two in the afternoon."

I didn't answer. I was still in school back then, and he didn't need to know we'd gotten out early that day. Though her blouse was disheveled and her hair messy, this mysterious chica made no move to straighten herself. Instead she kept her eyes fixed on me, as if I owed her an explanation.

"Diego—ah," my brother stammered. "This is my friend Violeta. She lives in Nuevo Laredo."

"*Hola*," I said.

"Ernesto," she said. "How come you didn't tell me you had a brother?"

"It didn't come up."

Her face was a smirk. "You hiding any others like him?"

"Just him."

"Good. I was beginning to think you were hiding a whole family of *guapos*."

I blushed. I was sixteen and had never had a woman call me handsome. She stood, straightened her T-shirt, and that's when she reached out and poked me in the chest. Suddenly, I knew what it was like to feel helpless.

"Well, it's nice to meet you, Diego, but now I have to go."

Ernesto followed her outside, where a brand-new Camaro was parked. As they kissed, she ran a finger down the front of his denim shirt. Then she got in the car and drove off, her tires spinning in the dust. Ernesto came back in, looking like he'd won the lottery. "What do you think of *that*, *hermano*?"

"Where'd you find her?"

"In a dance club. I was just standing there, talking to Miguel and Pancho, and she walked up to me."

"Just like that."

"Just like that. Batted her eyes. Gave me that look. It was like I was *chosen*."

"She's crazy. You know that, don't you?"

"You don't know the half of it. You should see her friends. Ay *cabrón*, I think I'm in love!"

And my thought was: Why you? Why do you get to fall in love? Why is that fair? Why, when you were the one who got caught stealing Mami's grocery money when you were eight years old? Why, when you were the one who snapped a guitar neck in half on the first day the school finally got musical instruments? Why, when you were the one who, while trying to smother a blaze you'd caused when playing with matches, set Mami's dish towels on fire? Why do you get to fall in love with a mad *chica* from Laredo who's a few years older and built like the Red Devil when I'm the one who always does everything he's supposed to? Why *is* that, Ernesto?

I'm brooding, just like Papi does, and that's when I spot my father walking along the roadway between towns. I blink several times and of course it's not Papi, it's just a poor Mexicano stumbling along the roadway. He's built like Papi, though, low and sturdy, his skin a dark teak. When the man hears me approach, he turns and sticks his thumb in the air.

I pull over and he jumps in.

"Ay *gracias*," he says. "It's hotter than the devil's ass out here. I'm Salvador." He sticks out his hand. It's warm and big and damp with sweat.

"Diego," I answer, forgetting that here I'm supposed to be Hector. I notice that his clothes, from his threadbare ball cap to his battered sneakers, are damp. "You swim across today?"

He throws his head back and laughs. "Ha! You got me! I've been walking all day. Thank God you picked me up, amigo. You'd think my clothes would be dry by now but it's so humid I think they're growing wetter, if anything."

"Where are you going?"

"A cotton field up ahead, just past Smithers. I'm what you call seasonal labor."

"Don't they give you some kind of card or something, saying you can enter the country?"

"Are you kidding? The good places do, but where I work I'm lucky if they pay me after they've taken off my room and board. Still, what are you going to do?"

Smithers looks exactly like every other small town I've passed through today: the same junked cars, the same slanting porches, the same blank gazes. "I take it you've crossed before?" I ask Salvador.

"Ay *si*. Many times. I come every fall. It's how I put food on the table back home. I have five children and, strangely enough, they expect to be fed. I'm from the south, *joven*. Chiapas." He looks out the window, and I can tell he's picturing home. "It's the most beautiful place on earth. In Chiapas you have everything— mountains, rivers, beautiful cities. We have Indians there who dress in these long, white robes and look like angels. Just talking about it makes me miss it already. It's the best place in the world. The only thing it doesn't have is jobs."

"That's too bad."

"Ay, *joven*, it's not your fault. Don't be feeling guilty for a mess you didn't make."

"I suppose. You shouldn't have to do this."

He's quiet for a moment. He's looking at me, his face all scrunched up. "How old are you?"

"Seventeen."

"Really? You look a bit older." He chuckles. "And since those are Mexican plates I figure I'm not the only one with a story to tell. Oh! I'm up here."

I spot a battered trailer in front of a field that stretches to the horizon. The air is thick with floating wisps of cotton. A group of men are standing around drinking out of those little plastic cups that are the tops of thermoses.

The Datsun backfires as I stop at the side of the road.

"*Gracias* again," Salvador says. "My feet were killing me."

"It's nothing."

"Oh! What do I owe you for the gas? Is a dollar fair? It was only a couple of miles."

I reach into my jeans and pull out the money Ernesto gave me. I peel off a ten-dollar bill and give it to him.

"Here. Take this."

"Oh no, I couldn't."

"Go on. You've got five kids to feed."

"That's no joke! Are you sure?"

He whoops when I shove the bill into his hand. "You see that! Do you see? Here I thought this day was going to be a complete loss. My clothes wouldn't dry, no one would give me a lift, my feet were killing me. And then you came along. You see, *joven*? You never can tell. Right when things are at their worst—bam! They get better. Good day, Diego. Maybe one day I'll see you down the road."

He gets out of the Datsun and walks toward the men in the field.

IT TAKES FOREVER to start Papi's car, the engine whirring and whirring while Salvador's work friends look over at me and laugh. Finally, the car starts with a stronger shudder than usual. I rev it hard so it doesn't stall and when it backfires loudly the men act like they've been hit with a pistol shot.

Ten minutes later, I have no choice but to take my chances on the ring road surrounding San Antonio, the car belching like a fat man who's had too many frijoles with his rice.

13

△▽△▽△▽

WITHIN MINUTES I'm surrounded by traffic. The Datsun can't keep up, so everybody's honking and then cutting in front of me, taking my lane away from me. I keep slowing down to leave space between me and the next driver, which only lets more drivers cut in front of me. At the same time, I'm looking for my exit and trying to get in the right lane and reading the traffic signs spanning the highway, and the whole time I'm thinking that if I crash, and the car is towed, I'll lose the package and my family will die.

I crank the wheel, drivers honking as I head for what I hope is the right exit. A minute later, I'm entering a neighborhood of dark three- and four-story buildings. There's graffiti everywhere, vibrant slashes of orange and yellow and green. Black guys my age are on every corner, calling out, "What you want? What you *need*?" The only other people on the street are skinny women with blank stares and blotchy skin, prowling along in high heels and tight clothing. At a stoplight, one comes up to the Datsun. She's smoking a cigarette and has a cheap plastic purse slung over a bony shoulder.

"How you doin' today, baby?" she asks just as the light turns green.

I step on the gas, thankful the car doesn't stall. Off in the distance I hear sirens. I pass a fire hydrant that's been opened. A bunch of kids—they all look nine or ten years old—are playing in the spray. I see an old man in rags talking to himself and a skinny old woman pushing a shopping basket filled with stuffed bags. I feel like I'm the only Mexican for miles and that's because I probably am.

I turn and I'm on the right street, and then I'm in front of the right building. After shutting off the engine, I turn the key halfway and pull up the parking brake. I hear a muffled clink and open the glove compartment. I put the package in the plastic bag that the cashier in Dilley—the one who reminded me of Violeta —used for my jerky and Coke. I take a deep breath.

The building is four stories high and covered with gang tags. Three young men are standing on the stoop, keeping watch. They're dressed in baggy shorts, brand-new Nike sneakers, and gold chains. I walk to the bottom of the three steps leading to the stoop, the bag clutched in my hand. My only hope is that with Papi's car it won't occur to anyone I'm carrying anything of value.

One of them says, "Nice car, Pedro."

I look up at him.

"Diego."

He lifts his shirt enough for me to see the pistol tucked into his pants. "Oh no you ain't. You come here in your luxury automobile, and you walk up to *my* building in *my* neighborhood, I'm gonna tell *you* what your name is, and far's I can tell it's Pedro."

The other two laugh. The third eyes me up and down, and says, "Man, what you want?"

"I want to see Crazy J," I say, hoping that my English holds up.

"How you know about Crazy J?" says the third man. "Mebbe they ain't no Crazy J here. You think of that?"

"El Tranquilo, he sent me."

They all stop laughing.

"Tranquilo sent you? You know him?"

"My brother is Ernesto Hernandez. He works for Mr. Tranquilo."

He squints at me, like he's trying to figure me out. "You shittin' me, man? Your brother's Ernesto?"

"*Si.*"

"He *look* like Ernesto," says one of the other two, a big guy with gold in his teeth.

"I know he look like Ernesto. What am I, blind?"

The first guy turns back toward me. "Where's Ernesto at?"

"He could not come. I have come in his place."

He looks at the other two. They both shrug their shoulders. The guy with the pistol pulls out an iPhone and, with his back turned, has a quick, mumbled conversation. "Ah right," he says when it's over. "Ah right. Go on in, Pedro ... sorry, *Diego* Hernandez. Seems they expectin' you. Ain't nobody told us, is all. Apartment 301. At the back. And don't be usin' the elevators. Ain't worked for years, know what I mean?"

"*Si,*" I tell him.

The other two snort, and one of them says, "Of course he sees. He *smart*. Any fool can see that. Just look at the *car* he be drivin'." This starts them all laughing hard and slapping each other's hands.

"Ah right, ah right," says the one in charge. "Well don't just stand there, Pedro or Diego or whatever your name is. Let's get the, uh, preliminaries over with."

"The ... what?"

"Spread your arms and legs, son. Assume the po-sition."

I put the bag at my feet. Then I part my legs and hold my arms outstretched. One of the flunkies steps forward and runs his hands over my chest and limbs and he even feels around my ankles. He grunts something, and I walk past them into the building. "And don't worry about your Ferrari," I hear one of them call out. "We'll keep an eye on it for you."

I WALK INTO A DARK HALLWAY. I can hear babies crying, TVs, and rap music. The hallway smells like old diapers and smoke. I pass the elevator—the door is half-open, and when I look in I can see it's littered with old paper and spilled food. Right beside is a door marked *Stairs*. I push it open and find the stairwell in shadows, every overhead light smashed, the bases of the broken bulbs still in the fixtures. The only light comes from little windows no bigger than boxes of cereal, placed high on each landing. At the next floor, I have to step over the legs of a skinny vago sitting against the wall of the stairwell. He's dressed in rags, a large rip down the front of his shirt. There's a needle on the step beside him; just as he's about to keel over, he wakens enough to snort and straighten himself. He looks up weakly. His eyes are watery and yellow. I keep moving.

I push open the door to the third floor and walk along the

100

hallway: it's exactly the same as the first floor, except there's more graffiti and more of the lights are punched out, shrouding the hallway in shadow. I reach the apartment. The door has been replaced by a thick piece of steel, the numbers 301 spray painted in red across it. There's a slit at eye level.

I knock. My knuckles barely make a noise against the thick metal so I knock harder, with the base of my palm. A pair of eyes appear behind the slit.

"You Diego?" says a voice.

"*Sí.*"

"Ernesto's brother?"

"*Sí.*"

I hear dead bolts slide open. The door swings wide and a young man wearing sunglasses and a red bandanna across the lower half of his face is pointing a gun in my face. He's holding the pistol sideways, like they do in the movies, and his finger is on the trigger. My heart hammers and I feel hot all over.

Breathe, *primo*. Breathe.

The gunman waggles the barrel, gesturing for me to come in. Inside, there's a battered sofa, a coffee table, and a matching chair. On the dingy walls are posters of Halle Berry and some rap group I don't know.

There's a skinny guy in the chair, looking at me. He's wearing a white T-shirt and jeans so baggy the crotch dips to his knees. Though he's barely older than I am, I can somehow tell it's Crazy J.

"This him, D?" he says to the gangster with the bandanna.

The other man nods.

"Take a seat."

I sit on the sofa. Crazy J watches, one eyebrow cocked.

"So," he says, "you Ernesto's little brother."

"*Si.*"

"It wasn't a question. I know who you is. That dope you got?"

I nod and put it on the table. He takes out the four bricks and looks at them. His right leg bounces nervously. Across his white T-shirt are the words *Crips Unite*.

"Why'd you come and not your brother?"

"He was in a car accident. He got a concussion."

"You tellin' me the truth?"

I nod.

"Well, lemme tell you something. Your boss, El Tranquilo, is on thin ice with me. First there's some trouble with his tunnels or some shit, and now I'm supposed to believe his main errand boy has clunked his head. That about the size of it, homes?" He leans forward, forearm across his knees. "It's unprofessional, know what I mean? You don't do *bizness* that way. They's plenty other places I can get my dope. Plenty other places more reliable. Them towel-heads, for one. Them *Afghanis*. Them mothers don't smoke, don't drink, don't do drugs, don't chase women. Even go to church. Mosque, they call it. You think they gonna screw up? No way. They as reliable as the rise and fall of the *sun*."

He leans back, and narrows his right eye at me.

"Course they dope ain't as good. Comes a longer way so it gets stepped on." He looks at the bricks. "Speakin' of dope … that the real deal?"

"*Si*," I tell him. I'm so scared I can't breathe. Crazy J looks at the gunman.

"You know what, D? We gonna test this shit. I ain't in a trusting mood tonight."

The gunman gets up, unlocks the steel door, and leaves. Crazy J just sits there, looking at me. Minutes go by. I feel like I'm going to throw up. I just want to get the money and leave this place forever.

"Tell me something, homes. You don't look like no gangster. You don't look like no dope slinger. Where you tattoos? Where you grill?"

"I am doing my brother a favor."

"So you don' wanna be no dope boy?"

"No."

"Then what you doin' here? What you doin' across the border, sellin' to a hard-core criminal like me? Plenty of better things you could do with your time. Things more productive, know what I mean?"

The question hangs between us. It's like the clanging of a bell, the echoes getting softer and softer but refusing to grow completely silent. The worst part of it is, I don't know whether he's serious or just messing with me or a little of both. Crazy J points a finger at my chest. "I'm gonna go out on a limb here, but I'm guessing things in Mexico just like they is up here. A few rich folk and everyone else poor as all get out? That the way things work down there?"

"Si."

His eyes bore into mine. "I got one other thing to say." He points toward the package with a finger. "If that dope don't meet my, uh, reasonable *expectations*, we gonna have ourselves a problem, you understand? You ain't walkin' outta here, mooo-chacho. The price we agreed on is for the real McCoy, *comprende?*"

I nod. The room is airless, and Crazy J's right leg keeps hopping up and down, like it's rigged with electricity. There's movement in the hallway—footsteps and people mumbling.

"About time," Crazy J mutters. He stands and walks to the thick metal door and begins sliding the dead bolts. "Where you been, boy? What take you so long?"

D steps into the room. For some reason, he's not wearing his bandanna, and when he speaks I can see his teeth are capped in gold. "These fools was hiding," he says. "Like rats in a alley."

"That figures. All day every day, they in your face, poundin' on doors, wanderin' the hallways, buggin' us for some of the black sludge and then on days we actually wants to *give* it to them they make themselves scarce. It don't make no sense but every time, it's the same damn thing."

D looks into the hallway and starts talking to whoever is out there. "Well, what you waiting for? We ain't got all *day* ... get your scrawny asses in here."

Five people shuffle into the room—four black men and one white woman. They're all skinny and sniffling, and the woman has bruises all over her legs. Their clothes smell bad, like milk turned sour.

"Come on, come on," says Crazy J. "You know the drill, sit yo' asses down."

The five move silently toward one wall. They're shaky and weak, and they keep wiping the undersides of their noses.

"What, I got to tell you to do everything?"

They sit, their backs against the wall, and look up at Crazy J

like children waiting for dessert. D disappears down the hallway and when he comes back he's got five needles, five bent spoons, and five lighters. He hands the needles and lighters out to the junkies. They take them eagerly, like the equipment itself is the drug.

Crazy J pulls a penknife out of his pocket and cuts into one of the bricks. Like Tranquilo said, the drug is black and gooey; without the confines of the package it even droops a little.

"Ah," Crazy J says while looking at me. "Mexico's finest, inn't that right dope boy?"

I shrug.

"You better hope it is, is all's I'm sayin'. I'm good and *tired* of Tranquilo's bullshit."

He puts a tiny dab on each spoon. Then he hands one to each of the addicts. I can't believe how quickly their shaky hands move, putting flames to the undersides of the spoons and then filling their syringes. It isn't like in *Trainspotting*, with the junkies sticking the needles into their outstretched forearms. The arms on these five people are a mass of scabs and scars, and my guess is they can't use them. One guy shoots into the back of his hand, hissing loudly when the needle strikes. Another rolls up a filthy pant leg and shoots into the top of his foot. The woman is the worst; she pulls out a compact mirror and uses it to shoot into the vein running up her neck.

They all issue loud sighs. Crazy J chuckles. "I think we *gettin'* somewhere," he says as the five loll against the wall. "What you think, D? We got uh-selves some real dope here?"

"We got some real dope here, boss."

"Well, ah right!" He's talking to the junkies. "On your feet."

The junkies struggle to get up. Their bodies are like rubber, their eyelids drooping. The white woman has the most trouble. She's sweating feverishly and a white, foamy spittle has formed at the corners of her mouth.

"All right!" says Crazy J. "I need some scores." He turns to the first addict. "You," he says.

"Nine."

"Whoo! A nine! What 'bout you?"

"Eight and a half, J."

"Eight point five. Dat respectable. I think maybe Tranquilo's come through for me. 'Bout time. *You.*"

Number three's head is rolling against the wall. His eyes are barely open. "Nine and a half." He sighs.

"Whoa! Nine point five. You hear dat shit! Now what about you?"

The fourth addict is grinning from ear to ear. Of the five, he's the only one who is steady on his feet. "What can I say? The shit is the *bomb*, J."

"Gimme a number."

"Ten. This shit's a ten! I tell ya, J, it's puttin' me on my *ass.*"

"You hear?!" says Crazy J. "We got a ten!" He turns to me. "Looks like you gonna get yourself paid, dope boy."

I'm not listening. The foam on the skinny white woman's mouth has turned slightly green. Blood is bubbling up from the spot where she injected herself, and her knees have started to wobble. I'm about to say something, like maybe she needs help, when she drops. It doesn't look like a person tripping. Her arms don't go out or anything, she just plummets full weight and hits the floor hard.

D goes up to the woman and puts his hand over the woman's mouth. He looks up, grinning, his mouth a mix of gold and teeth. "Bitch is still breathin', boss."

"Well, get her outta here. Last thing we need is dead bodies in our crib." He turns to me. "Now. You tell Tranquilo that him and me, we back in *biz*ness! You tell him we ah *right* again! That gotta be some crazy stuff to put out Stacey's lights!" He turns to the junkies. "Well, what you waitin' for? Go on, job's over, you done got what you wanted, so *out!*"

They shuffle out, three of them barely able to walk while the fourth is singing happily to himself. D grabs Stacey's feet and drags her away, and where he takes her I don't know.

I can't help it: "Will she be all right?"

"What … Stacey? Sure she be ah right. She hard-core, you know what I mean? Besides, what do you care?"

Crazy J gets up and leaves. I'm alone and shaky and wishing I'd seen none of this. Crazy J comes back into the room with a small Nike bag, like the kind gringos use to carry tennis stuff.

"Here," he says.

I open the zipper. The bag is packed with money.

"Don't count it. You don't wanna insult me. It's all there."

I stand and walk toward the thick metal door. I open it and am about to step into the hallway when I pause.

"Go on," J says. "You don't have to worry. Word's out you wit me. Ain't nobody gonna mess wit you. Leastways not in this neighborhood. You go a little east of here, that's Blood territory, I can't vouch for shit. But here you gon' be ah right."

I nod.

"And one other thing. I knows you now. Next time, we ain't

gotta go through none ah this. All this bullshit, all this suspicion, it's cause I didn't know you. But now I do. You hear me? Next time, we get to *expedite* the process, know what I mean? You done good, dope boy. You a natural."

I walk out of the building. People look at me and they know I'm carrying a bag full of bundled cash and nobody says or does anything. There are two kids, each is maybe ten years old, standing around the Datsun. They just stand there, looking up at me.

"The car's safe," says one of them in a little voice.

I nod. They don't leave. Then I realize they'd been assigned to watch the car. I reach into my pocket and pull out the money Ernesto gave me. I hand them ten dollars. They take it and run off.

I get in the car. The Nike bag's too big for the secret compartment, so I stash it under the passenger seat.

If I get the money back to Mexico, Ernesto will live. We'll all live.

It's as simple as that.

14

▲▽▲▽▲▽

THE DATSUN STARTS AS IT ALWAYS DOES, coughing up blue smoke and shaking before finally settling down. I pull away and try to find my way to the highway. All I have to do is drive back the way I came, though I keep hitting one-way streets that run the wrong way. The highway looks about five blocks away, though when I head toward it I'm turned away after a single block and that's when I start trembling. It comes on suddenly, like a bracing chill. I can't help it. I'm picturing the white woman in Crazy J's drug den, the way the froth bubbled up from the corner of her mouth, and then I'm seeing those corpses out on the highway next to Corazón, and then I hear the buzzing of flies in my ears. I pull over and the car stalls and I rest my forehead on the grooved steering wheel while taking deep, racking breaths. The air entering my lungs smells like damp cloth and old food and oil.

I hear footsteps. I open my eyes, and there's an old man moving in front of the car. He's walking slowly, shuffling almost, and if he notices me he doesn't show it. His pants are grimy and he's not wearing a shirt and he has a bandage on his upper arm, like he's been in an accident. I close my eyes and breathe and when I open them again I see Ernesto, shuffling toward the kitchen late one night, a bandage on his upper arm, about a year ago.

He was stumbling and giggling to himself, and when Mami heard him she rushed out of her bedroom, her nightgown gathered at her throat. Papi and I were both watching television in the living room.

"Ernesto!" she cried. "Where have you been? We were worried sick."

"Mami," he said, "I told you, I was visiting some friends in Nuevo today."

"*Hijo* ... are you sure?"

"Don't you remember? Violeta's birthday?"

"Are you hungry?"

"Ay, *si*. I'll never say no to your stuffed chilies."

Papi's chair creaked. I looked over and saw him rising from his seat, going toward Ernesto. He pointed to the bandage on Ernesto's upper arm.

"What happened?" Papi asked.

"It's nothing," said Ernesto. The two of them stared at each other, like the first one who blinked would lose the contest, and I thought of the time Papi got so mad at Ernesto for standing up on the Red Devil. This time, instead of slapping Ernesto, Papi reached out and grabbed a corner of the bandage and tore it clean off. Ernesto howled. Even through the blur of antiseptic cream you could see it was a tattoo of a young woman with dark curls and a round face and a hard look about her.

Papi threw the bandage to the floor. "No!" he shouted. "I won't have it!"

"Eduardo," Mami cried. "Don't get so mad. All the kids are getting tattoos these days."

"Not of *her*," Papi spat.

Ernesto smirked. "Relax, Papacito, it's just a little ink …"

"You know what I'm talking about, Ernesto."

"Eduardo stop it!"

"You ask him," he shouted at Mami. "Go ahead."

Mami did no such thing; she went to the kitchen while Ernesto smirked away. Papi grabbed his jacket and marched toward the door. Just before leaving the house, he paused and peered at me for a few seconds. It was like he was asking me a question.

I'm sixteen, I wanted to tell him. I like rock music and hamburgers. I like staying up late and watching movies. Ernesto's different, I wanted to tell him.

You don't have to worry about me.

I PUT THE DATSUN IN GEAR and start looking for the highway again. One neighborhood shifts into another. The graffiti is now in Spanish. The muchachos hanging on the street corners have brown skin and baggy pants and bandannas tied around their shaved heads. Their eyes follow me as I crawl by. A few call out to me, "*Oye, primo, qué quieres? Qué necessitas?*" and I try not to look.

I keep driving. The car window is open against the heat. I can hear cumbia music and people shouting. I still can't find the highway, and after a bit more driving I spot an older woman standing at the side of a street, clutching a purse in both hands. She's wearing ugly beige shoes, like the kind nurses wear, and a ratty green overcoat that's buttoned all the way up to her throat. I decide she's Honduran or Guatemaltecan and not Mexican, maybe because there's something different looking about her that I don't quite understand. Meanwhile, she's staring straight ahead, both hands crossed over her stomach, her jaw moving in small circles, like a cow eating its cud. Her dentures, I figure.

I stop driving. The Datsun shakes and shudders and spits blue smoke. I lean over and call, "Señora?" through the passenger-side window.

She continues staring straight ahead.

"Señora?" I call again, a little bit louder.

When she ignores me I step out of the car. This gets her attention. She looks at me with blazing eyes, and for a moment I consider getting back in Papi's crappy little car and driving away.

"Can you tell me how to get to the highway?" I ask, happy to be using Spanish again.

She starts nodding her head. Her eyes focus on me, though she still doesn't speak. Her jaw never stops moving.

Then she points across the street. "*Por ahí*," she says.

I follow her outstretched finger to a stretch of sooty wall. It's covered with gang tags and Spanish swear words. "*Ahí*," she says again, as if she's seeing something and it's making her worried.

"Señora, do you need some help?"

"It all happened right there. I was just standing here, minding my own business, when *he* appeared in a ring of smoke."

"Who, señora?"

Her eyes flash on mine. They're pinpricks, fixed on me. "It was

Satan himself, *hijo*. *El diablito*. Come to take the world for his own pleasure. He was right there, grinning like a happy baby, it was going to be so *easy* for him. So I yell. Make a noise. Throw things. The devil doesn't like that, *sabes*? He prefers to be undercover. His biggest trick is pretending he doesn't exist. You know that, don't you? But I got the jump on him! He frowned and disappeared and from what I can figure that bit of wall over there must be some kind of gateway to his underworld. So that's why I'm here. Waiting. If he comes again I'll *catch* him."

She makes a motion like a man snagging a housefly in midair. Her bony fist hovers and, if I'm not mistaken, her jaw starts rotating in the opposite direction.

"Señora. Do you know how to get to the highway?"

"There isn't any highway near here. You must be lost."

"I am," I tell her.

I get back in the Datsun and drive away. After a while, I find myself in a neighborhood of tidy little houses. Gone are the graffiti and broken glass. The people are a mix of black and white and Latino. When I pass they look at me, their expressions saying they're on their guard. Finally, I spot signs directing traffic to the highway. I make a left, a right, a left, and when I get to the on-ramp I hit the gas and pray the old Datsun makes it. It shakes like a mambo dancer. It coughs like a heavy smoker. My foot is hard on the accelerator and the merge lane is about to end and I'm still not up to highway speed. I look for a gap in the lane next to me and, at the last moment, squeeze between a delivery van and a crappy box-shaped sedan. The sedan driver honks, and I don't care. I've done it, the money's beneath the seat and I just have to cross back over the border. Do they have dogs that can smell

American cash? Does gringo cash *have* a smell? If they don't it'll be easy because no one but no one ever gets stopped going *into* Mexico.

As soon as possible I find a country road that's heading in the direction of the border and I leave the highway. Soon it veers, and as far as I can tell I'm parallel to the border, heading toward the crossing at Eagle Pass. I keep driving. It's like I have two layers of vision. One that sees what's really in front of me: ramshackle houses and fields of cotton and the odd slow-moving truck. The other is like a crazy movie, playing over the things that are really there, and in this movie I can see Ernesto's new linked-*C* tattoo, and the defeated expression Papi wears on his face all the time, and Crazy J throwing back his head and laughing, *ha ha ha ha ha ha ha*, when that woman named Stacey dropped to the floor.

Only it isn't Crazy J laughing. It's a strange new sound the Datsun is making, halfway between a rattle and a clunk, and when the motor cuts out I veer to the side of the road, slowly coming to a stop next to a field planted with some crop I don't recognize. Maybe it's canola or soybean or whatever. All I know is the Datsun has died in the middle of nowhere.

I get out. I pop the hood. Though I know nothing about motors or how they work, I take a look anyway. Nothing seems broken, so I get back in the car and try to start it. The starting motor whirrs and whirrs and then goes silent. I turn the key once again and there's nothing but the stench of roasting oil, and after a minute that goes away too.

I look in every direction. There are fields and a long patchy roadway. I can't even see any houses from where I'm standing.

In my head, I add up all that I know. The first thing is I'm smuggling a bag full of money, lots and lots of money, into Mexico. The second thing is the car is dead. The third thing is if the police come by and find a broken-down car with Mexican plates at the side of the road, they're bound to ask questions.

I reach under the seat and grab the money and take off into a field full of cotton pods. All I know is I'm running as fast as I can, taking high awkward steps so I don't trip on the plants. Sweat is streaming into my eyes. My hair and clothes are covered with white fluff. With each heaving breath I can feel cotton spores getting into my lungs. I stop and bend over and start coughing, and when I'm done I stand up and take stock.

I'm in the middle of the field. All I can see is blue sky and rows and rows of cotton. I hear a large motor running somewhere far off; probably someone's tractor. I've run far enough that I can't see the car or the road, and without another plan I open the bag and pull out one of the bundles of cash. It's American fifties, and I quickly count twenty in the bundle. Then I dump out the bag into a hollow of crushed cotton plants and, crouching down, count the bundles.

There's a hundred thousand dollars, just lying at my feet. I stand there staring at it, then stuff it all back in the bag. I start walking. I have no plan. I just walk. It's searingly hot, and I wish I had a hat and some water. I come to a road. I see the Datsun, about a kilometer away. In all that time, I've done nothing but walk in a huge semicircle. The only thing I've accomplished is exhausting myself, so I lean over and catch my breath and call myself a stupid *pendejo* over and over and over. Finally, I straighten, and do the only thing I *can* do, which is tromp back into the field and try to walk in a direction that carries me far away from the car.

Before I do, I happen to look up. Off in the distance, well past Papi's junked Datsun, I see a vehicle approaching. As it gets closer, I can tell it's a nice car, a BMW in fact, and I wonder what it's doing out on these back roads, where most of the cars have rusty doors and rattling exhaust pipes. I stick out my thumb even though I know it's pointless. In America, people don't pull over for poor Mexican teenagers covered in cotton fluff.

But they do. The car comes to a stop just ahead of me, and the passenger-side window rolls down. There's a pretty blond *chica* and she's drinking a Tecate. Beside her, at the wheel, is a grinning college boy with long brown hair and a University of Texas T-shirt. In the backseat is another scrawny white kid, and he's wearing one of those big caps that Bob Marley used to wear to keep his dreadlocks out of his face when he played football.

"Hiya," says the girl. "Y'all want a lift?"

I nod. My throat is dry and I feel dizzy.

"Well, don't just stand there. Get in!"

For some reason, this makes all three of them laugh and already I'm uncomfortable. I get in anyway, the driver peeling away as soon as I close my door. For a moment, the car is clouded in dust and fine gravel and then the air clears. They're listening to some kind of music without singing, just a lot of guitar playing that goes on and on and on. The girl turns.

"My name's MaryLou," she says. Once again the other two laugh. With her opened Tecate, she gestures toward the driver. "This here's Sal, and that juvenile delinquent in the back is Dean."

There are more titters. I think maybe these aren't their real names, that it's some joke they're leaving me out of.

MaryLou looks at me. She's a beauty who knows it.

"What's yer name, hon?"

"Diego."

"And I'm guessing, Diego, that you're from Mexico?"

"*Si*. I mean, yes. I am."

The driver, Sal, looks at me in his rearview mirror. "I hear they got liquor down there has a *worm* at the bottom of the bottle, and if you eat this worm, man ..." He makes a funny motion with his hand. "You gonna trip hard. That true, Diego? You ever eat the worm."

"No," I tell them. "It is not true."

"Hey Diego," says MaryLou. "This is your lucky day. Y'all wanna know *why*?"

"Okay."

"It's your lucky day because, as y'all can plainly see, I'd just opened myself a nice cold Tecate when I spotted you at the side of the road. And I said to Sal and Dean, 'Hey, I just opened a Mexican beer, and there's a Mexican dude needing a lift. Gotta be a sign. Let's give him a lift.'"

Dean grins. Sal bursts with laughter, holding his face. "Y'all wanna beer yourself?" MaryLou asks.

"Okay."

There must be a cooler at her feet since the bottle she passes me is so cold it's dripping with condensation. I untwist the top and take a good long swallow. She hands one to Dean and then one to Sal; he holds his bottle with one hand while steering with the other.

"So," says MaryLou. "Where y'all goin'?"

"Back to Mexico."

"Well, we can drop you off at one of the crossings if you'd like. Couldn't we, Sal?"

"We could. We aren't on any schedule I can think of."

"That would be good."

"Well, all right then!"

"Where are you going?" I ask them.

"Here, there, everywhere. We're on the road, really." The two college boys chuckle. It's like everything MaryLou says is funny. "Seriously, now that school's over we're just, like, wandering. We may find our way to Burning Man. You know, in Nevada? But we don't know. That's the thing, *we just don't know*. It ain't like we're going to find jobs or anything, not these days."

MaryLou turns in her seat and places a foot on the dashboard; she's wearing low-rise Keds, and there's a ring of dirt around her ankle. Her legs are long and tanned and thin.

"Yup," she says. "We're just gonna let the wind blow us. Maybe we'll drive into Mexico." She turns to look at me again. "You think we should do that, hon? Drive into Mexico?"

I shrug.

"I went once with my parents. Course, we flew. To the Playa del Riviera. You know it?"

"I have heard of it."

"You gotta go!" She giggles. "I had, like, the best time there. Except my folks were with me. But they have these ruins there? Tulum, Chichen Itza, we took little trips. Did you *know* ..." She turns around all the way and props herself on her knees, her forearms resting on the back of the seat. She's looking right at me, grinning. "Did you know the priests used to, like, sacrifice virgins? As, like, a sacrifice to the gods?"

"You'd be safe then," says Sal, causing Dean to fold up laughing.

"Very funny!" MaryLou says as she turns and sits back down. She props a foot on the dashboard, right against the dusty footprint she left last time she put her foot up.

That's when I hear crinkling beside me. It's Dean. He's taking a plastic baggie out of his hoodie pocket and now I know why they're all giggling. He starts rubbing some *mota* between his thumb and forefinger, letting it drop into a rolling paper he's balanced on his knee. MaryLou looks back and notices.

"Dean! Are you *kidding* me? Not again!"

"Hey, we got a guest. We gotta make him feel, like, *welcome*."

"Plus," says Sal, "if we're gonna cross some borders we're gonna have to get rid of it anyway."

Dean lights up and passes the burning *mota* to me. It smolders away under my nose, smelling like sweet tar. If I could punch that proud smirk off his face I would. My feet tighten against the bag of money at my feet.

"Hey man," says Dean. "What's your problem?"

"Yeah, man," says Sal. "Chill."

"Maybe he doesn't smoke?" says MaryLou as she reaches for the burning spliff. "That it, hon? You a nonsmoker?"

Again. That communal giggle. I hear MaryLou inhaling. It sounds like air escaping a bicycle tire. She passes the *hierba* to Sal, who takes a full draw and passes it back to Dean.

"Maybe Diego's afraid of getting caught! That it, man? You afraid of the law?" MaryLou giggles, and looks over the headrest at me. Even her prettiness bothers me. It's like another thing that's been given to her, yet another bit of good fortune she didn't have to work for. I imagine her parents—you see them on gringo TV shows all the time, the stockbroker father, the mother in pearl earrings, the dog a golden retriever. I'd bet she has a brother on a football team somewhere.

"Man, you should've looked at the plates on this car a bit closer," Sal says with a laugh. "Those, amigo, are diplomatic plates, courtesy of my old man. If some trooper stopped this car, I could have his ass for, like, breakfast."

"Yeah man. I bet we've got the only car in the world with, like, diplomatic plates next to a Phish sticker."

Again, the laughter.

"Stop the car," I order.

"Huh?" says Sal.

"Stop it. I want to get out."

They realize I'm not joking. Dean gives me a wounded look, like I've ruined some game they've been playing.

"Look, Diego," says MaryLou. "We're just letting our hair down a little, ya know? Like, we were studying hard for our finals. They went on for like two weeks. There's nothing wrong with having a little fun—"

I can feel my face turning red. The blood is pounding in my temples. "Pull this car over now."

"All right, all right," says Sal.

The tires hit the gravel shoulder. "You sure, man?" says Sal. "I'd hate to leave you stranded out here."

I grab the bag at my feet and open the door and step out. Beside me, I can hear the passenger-side window hum down. "Diego," MaryLou says. "You sure you gonna be all right?"

I start walking. They're following along beside me. They can't believe this is happening. They can't believe they can't make any of this right.

"Diego," MaryLou says again. "Are you *sure*?"

"*Si*," I tell them. "I have friends who live near here."

"Ohhh," she says, "well in that case … adios, Diego!"

The car peels away, kicking gravel onto the toes of my boots. I look around. I really am in the middle of nowhere. There's nothing but desert scrub on either side of me. The back of my neck feels like it's already burning in the sun. My mouth feels dry, and I wish I had water. All I can think about is the bag of money I have in my hand, and how I should have put up with those three spoiled morons at least for a while longer. Out here, I'm exposed. Anyone could pull over and want to know what I'm doing out here. That's when I notice a spindly little path, leading south from the roadway.

If I had to make a guess, I'd say it's headed toward the river.

15

△▽△▽△▽

I'M SURROUNDED BY PRICKLY PEAR CACTI and low, gnarled mesquite trees. I keep disturbing sidewinders and desert voles and little olive-green lizards. They scurry past my boot tips and blend with the terrain. The path is littered with empty plastic water bottles and old tortilla wrappers and bits of cellophane messed with sandwich crumbs. As far as I can tell, I've happened on a path used by *indocumentados* entering or leaving the United States. Whether this makes me lucky or not I don't know.

The river is far off—I can't yet see it—though if I follow this path I know I won't end up walking in circles. So I keep going. It's late in the afternoon and soon the sun will start to dip, casting the desert in a purple shadow. I have no food, no water, nothing to protect the bag of money when I swim. My lousy cell phone doesn't even get a signal out here. If I had any sense, I'd turn around and head back to the road and try to find a store and buy provisions for a long desert hike. For a moment I even stop, though after a few seconds, I start moving again. At least here I'm hidden by all this scrub.

The sun starts to sink a little, the intense heat of the day turning to a tolerable warmth. My shirt is damp against my back. That's where I'll feel the cold when the sun is all the way down. I keep marching and marching and after an hour I start to wonder whether I've made a mistake and maybe the road I left wound around without my noticing and really I'm heading away from the border. I stop and breathe and look in every direction, wishing I had some clue. Again, I think about turning back, but I figure if I keep going and still can't get to the river, I can find someplace to curl up and shiver away the night and then walk back to the road in the morning.

And then, like that, the river comes into view, a ribbon of red-brown about a half hour's walk away. Then again, distances are tricky over flat, featureless land, so it might be more.

I keep going, spurred by relief. After a while, I notice a shack made of tacked-together one-by-six planks up ahead. An old man, shaky and bony, steps out and peers at me. I realize he's manning a store that sells supplies to people crossing into or out of *el norte*. I start to think my plan could work.

"Crossing today, *joven*?"

"*Si*," I answer. "I'm going home."

"Everyone's coming back home these days. No more jobs in the U.S., isn't that right?" He laughs, his frail shoulders bobbing. "I don't know what the gringos will do when we're all gone. Who'll mow their lawns and take care of their kids?"

"They might have to do it themselves."

He smiles widely, and I see that his mouth contains only a few peggy orange teeth. "Pretty soon the gringos will start guarding the border to prevent us from leaving. You need supplies, *hijo*?"

"*Si.*"

"What do you need?"

I look at the goods on the shelves behind him. "I'll take some tortillas, some water, some chips."

He turns and puts those items in a plastic bag.

"And I need a backpack."

"Ay *si*," he says. "You do at that. The only problem is, I don't sell backpacks."

"Really? What about that one?" I point to a dusty old knapsack on the floor of the cabin.

"That one's mine."

"I really need it."

"I know that, *compadre*. But it's not for sale."

"I have money."

"I'd have to charge you twenty gringo dollars. And I'm telling you, the thing's years old and is fraying at the seams. It's not worth two dollars. But it's mine so I'd need twenty."

"Then twenty's what I'll give you."

He peers at me. One eye narrows. His face is a crisscross of wrinkles and lines. "Now why would a rich young man like yourself need to swim back into Mexico?"

"Maybe I want the exercise."

He gives me that smile again, all pink gums and awful teeth. "Well, then, it looks like we have a deal."

He upends the knapsack, and I watch a sandwich wrapped in cellophane, a can of Coca-Cola, a flashlight, and a small pistol tumble to his feet. He sees me eyeing the gun. "An old man can't be too careful," he says. "Not out here, all by himself. But don't worry, *hijo*. I got the safety on. But I tell you. Ain't nobody in their right mind going to mess with me."

"I'll need one more plastic bag, if that's all right."

"*Como no*? Plastic's cheap." He pulls one off a roll and sticks it in the backpack along with the stuff I've just bought.

"*Gracias*."

"*De nada*," he says. "We'll call it twenty-five even, okay?"

I nod. I've spent all of the *plata* Ernesto gave me, so I reach into the bag from Crazy J. The first bill I touch is worth fifty dollars, so I hand it to the old man. He eyes the money as if it's toxic. "What do you think I am? El Banco de México? I can't change this ..."

"You don't have to," I say. "Keep it. Good night, señor."

He looks like he might break into a dance. "Good night, *joven*. And watch out for snakes! They're the size of fire hoses out there!"

I MOVE ALONG THE PATH leading to the banks of the river, the old man's pack on my back and the bag full of money in my right hand. The old man goes back inside his teetering shack so I stop and pack the money in the extra plastic bag. Then I stuff it into the knapsack as well and throw the Nike bag as far as I can into the desert. When I put the knapsack back on, it feels swollen against my spine.

The sun slips beneath the horizon. I walk faster, knowing that darkness comes on quickly in the desert: one moment the earth is a soft purple, the next it's pitch-black. Pretty soon I'm stumbling along in the dark, my feet scuffling against dead earth. I look back. Way off, the old man has lit a torch. It's the only light I have, the moon lost behind dark, chunky clouds, though every once in a while the clouds part and I see moonlight glimmer off the river up ahead. This keeps me going in the right direction, though when the moon loses itself altogether it's like a thin blanket has been thrown over my head. I can't even see the old man's light anymore, probably because he's closed up for the night. The only thing I can do is feel my way along while struggling to stay calm. When my boots are on the path, they make a soft, swooshing sound, like bare feet on a beach. When I step off the path, I hear the crunch of weeds and scrub and low desert plants. My only other clue is the gurgle of the river, coming from somewhere ahead.

With nothing to look at, my eyes are making out shapes that don't really exist, squares and triangles and then circles that morph into human faces: Ernesto and Tranquilo and then Papi, always Papi, his face flickering sad and defeated in front of me. Pretty soon my ears start making noises too. They're loud enough to drown out the sounds of the river and of my feet striking the path and this frightens me. I hear Mami getting on my back for sleeping in so late. I hear Ernesto telling me to be more like him. I hear Tranquilo saying how clever I was to drive such a crappy car, and this triggers Papi's tired voice: *Ay hijo, you know I took your mother on our first date in this car? Did you know that, Diego?*

Papi's voice disappears. In its place I hear water. The clouds above part and let some moonlight through and I can see I'm on the banks of the *río*, at a little homemade campsite. There's a fire pit with an old coffeepot on a grate. There's a little lean-to, built of huisache twigs and twine. There's garbage everywhere. I look around to make sure I'm alone. Though there are shapes in the darkness, I'm pretty sure none of them are human.

"*Hola?*" I call to make sure. "Is anyone there?"

There's no answer.

I walk toward the lean-to and crawl beneath the canopy, wrapping the straps of the knapsack around my legs; this way, if someone comes along they can't steal it while I sleep. I curl up, making myself as small as possible. Already it's starting to get cold and I know it's only going to get colder. I'm not a good swimmer and I can't help but worry about crossing the river. My heart's pounding. It's like a fist striking wood, like someone angrily knocking on a door, *bang bang bang bang bang*, and a second later I'm not at the riverbank anymore. I'm alone in my house in Corazón, about a year ago.

I got up and opened the door. There she was, breathing hard, mascara trickling down her cheeks, her eyes spinning pinpricks.

"Where's Ernesto?"

"He's not here."

"You're lying!" she screeched, her eyes gone wide like a madwoman. "I know he's here, with that *puta* of his!"

"No, Violeta, *por favor*, he's out somewhere—"

She gave me a shove and then she was inside the house, storming into our bedroom, yelling, "Ernesto! I know you're here!" When she ran into Mami and Papi's bedroom I went after her and chased her back into the main room of the house. She charged into the kitchen and started throwing things to the floor—egg flippers, cutlery, an old plastic jug—while crying and yelling and swearing she was going to kill him.

"Violeta," I yelled. "Stop it. I'll go get him."

She wiped the underside of her nose. Milk dripped from a tilted jug in her hand.

"You know where he is?"

"*Sí*. I think so. Wait here."

She slumped at the kitchen table and put her face in her hands. "Oh Diego … he's replaced me with some teenager! You should see her, the little tramp."

Ernesto's two best friends in town were named Miguel and Pancho. I went to Pancho's house first and found the lights off. Then I headed to Miguel's, on a quiet block near the *palacio municipal*. I could see the three of them through the living room window, drinking beer and laughing. Tupac's *Thug Life* was seeping into the street.

I knocked on the window. When they didn't hear me, I knocked harder. They all looked up.

"Hey!" yelled Pancho. "It's that kid brother of yours!"

"Maybe he wants a beer. He want a beer, Ernesto?"

Ernesto shook his head and came outside. He was staggering a little and his eyes were bloodshot. He blinked in the sunlight.

"*Hermano*," he said. "*Qué pasa?*"

"Ernesto, you gotta come. Violeta's at the house."

His eyes narrowed. "Why didn't you tell her I wasn't home?"

"I did! She's crazy and on drugs. Thank God Mami and Papi are at the market. One second she's tearing the place apart, and now she's at the table, crying into her hands. You got a mess on your hands, *cabrón*."

When we got to the house I started to follow Ernesto inside. He stopped me. "This don't concern you," he said.

I watched through a break in the living room curtains. Violeta was still hunched over the table, her face lost behind a curtain of dark hair. He put a hand on her back and she slapped it away. Though I couldn't hear what Ernesto was saying, his tone was soft, almost pleading. I leaned a little closer, my ear touching the glass. This is what I heard: "But you know you're the only woman for me … you know you're my *amor*, my *corazón*, my everything …"

Violeta lifted her face. She looked like she'd been rained on by ink. He put a hand on her back again and this time she let it stay. They got up and left and I didn't see my brother for three days.

I was in my hammock, trying to sleep, when he came back whistling. He took off his clothes and lay down. We were both just looking up at the ceiling, the hammocks swinging from side to side.

"Ernesto," I said.

"*Qué?*"

"You're fooling around on Violeta, aren't you?"

"Of course."

"Not smart. She's out of her mind."

"You're right there, *hermano*. But don't worry. There isn't a woman on this earth I don't know how to handle. Besides, I'd have to be crazy to break up with her. Her uncle's going to give me a job. And not a lousy maquiladora job, either. One that pays crazy money, amigo."

"Her uncle?"

"Ay *si*. He's a businessman in Laredo. A powerful one."

"What's his name?"

"Juan Riesgo. But no one calls him that. Instead they call him by his nickname."

"Which is?"

Ernesto interlaced his fingers behind his head, as if all the cares in the world didn't apply to him. "They call him El Tranquilo. The Quiet One."

16

▲▽▲▽▲▽▲▽

MY EYES OPEN. The air is cold and the light's weak. My muscles ache from shivering all night long. The first thing I do is reach between my knees to check that the backpack is still there. Then I pull out the packet of tortillas and the can of Coke. I peel off one of the tortillas and, still lying on my side, start to chew. As soon as I'm finished eating, I'll swim for it.

The only problem is I don't know where I am. Even if I had an iPhone instead of my crappy old Nokia cell phone, it wouldn't matter since I can't get a signal out here. On the other side of the river, there could be several days' worth of desert to cross before I reach the border highway, or there could be a hundred meters. I suppose I'll find out soon.

I sit up and take a swig of warm Coca-Cola. The sun is rising quickly. From within the lean-to, I can see it lifting away from the horizon. I crawl out and piss on a prickly pear, the sun warming my face. The river is fairly narrow—about the width of a football pitch—and I figure I'll make it to the other side even if I have to dog-paddle.

Just as I'm zipping up, I hear tires on packed scrub.

A rattling old truck crests the top of the riverbank and stops, the motor belching before jiggling to a rest. The door opens and a man steps out. He's bigger than me and has tattoos running up and down his exposed, leathery arms. His eyes are covered by wraparound sunglasses and his beard is so long that he's knotted it with thick rubber bands, so that it looks like a length of red-brown rope. He's wearing a tattered ball cap, khaki pants, military boots, and a vest with the American flag on it. Or at least I think it's the American flag—when I look a little closer, I notice three columns in the top left corner, like the Roman numeral for *three*, surrounded by a circle of stars. Underneath the flag is another patch, this one reading, *FROM MY COLD DEAD HANDS*.

The man moves toward me and I start to shake. He's carrying an assault rifle the size of a small dog. I've seen AK-47s in news reports about guns found in cartel hideouts, and I'm pretty sure I'm looking at one now. He stops about ten feet away.

"You don't belong here."

"I am sorry."

"Your type shouldn't come here."

"Don't worry. I am leaving."

"You're leavin' all right."

I bend over, lift my knapsack and slip it over my shoulders. With my hands up, I start backing toward the river.

"Hey!" he yells. "Where you think you're going?"

"I'm swimming back to Mexico. In a few seconds I will be gone."

He smiles, showing tin in his teeth. I'm still trembling.

"No you ain't. I let you cross and you'll just come back over when I ain't around. That business don't wash here anymore, amigo. There's a new dawn coming."

"I will not return," I tell him. "I promise you, sir."

"Damn straight you won't. Now, this here's the way it's gonna be. Me an' some of my boys are camped just along the way, and that's where you and me are going. We picked up a few others of your kind and y'all are going to get a little talking to."

I swallow. It's like he's a soldier in some militia that has something to do with America, but at the same time doesn't. He lowers the barrel of his gun so that it's pointed at the middle of my chest. I try not to think about what it would do to me.

"This used to be a great country," he grunts. "Best in the damn world."

He reaches inside a pocket of his khakis and pulls out a pair of handcuffs. He holds them up, the chain looped over a fat, pink forefinger.

"Turn around."

"No. I am swimming, sir."

"Turn around," he says through gritted teeth.

I face the river. I could run for it and dive in the water, but with a gun like his I'd be full of holes before I took two strokes.

"Hands behind your back."

My legs feel light, like they're made from air. I hear his boots shuffle in the scrub.

"Now you put those hands together, boy."

"Okay, okay."

I look over my shoulder as he unsnaps the cuffs. As he walks toward me, the rifle barrel tips up, just a little, so that it's point-ed at a space above my shoulder. Everything slows—it's like I'm watching myself as I throw my fist forward and then draw it back hard to elbow him in the nose. The sound of bone cracks like a gunshot.

His hands go to his face and I grab the weapon. I take a few steps and fling it with all my might into the river. Then I turn back and look at him. We're both breathing hard. His nose is bleeding, and I know his head must be spinning. That's the thing about a punch to the nose: it'll take the fight out of pretty much anyone.

He's hunched over, still catching his breath, blood dripping onto his hand. He stands straight up, his face almost purple. When he smiles, blood spills down his upper lip and into his mouth, turning the space between his teeth red. He looks up to the sky, howls, and then charges, running full steam like some gringo football running back. I have time for one punch and it lands on the top of his head where there's nothing but hard bone. I hear my knuckles crack and then I'm down and he's on top of me and his huge hands find their way around my throat.

My air is gone. My eyes are bulging. As his blood drips onto my shirt, he says, in the coldest voice I've ever heard, "You're gonna pay for that."

Things are going black around the edges. His face is starting to waver, like I'm seeing it in a reflection. I have ten or twenty sec-onds of air left, and that's when I remember something Ernesto told me, something you should do if your opponent's on top and you're really taking it good. With my right hand I form a fist with my thumb out. With my left hand I grab his knotted beard and yank his face toward me while I punch that thumb as hard as I can into his eye. He screams and rolls off me and then I'm on my feet, running toward the river. I dive into the cold water and start swimming as hard as I can. I'm sure he's going to come after me, but when I pause and look back over my shoulder he's still rolling on the sandy sloping riverbank.

I can barely breathe. My throat feels compressed and I can't draw air and my boots are filling with water. I reach down and pull off my boots, letting them sink to the bottom of the Rio Bravo. This helps, and I start swimming again. A quick look back tells me that the militiaman is now on his feet, a hand over his eye and his nose like a bloody spigot.

"This ain't over!" he yells. "I'll be waitin', ya wetback, I'll be goddamn waitin'!"

I keep swimming—or at least my version of swimming; it's more like I'm flailing my arms and feet while trying to keep afloat—and the whole time I'm thankful the Rio Bravo is so narrow. The man's voice grows fainter and fainter, until finally it's replaced by the gurgle of water in my ears. My arms and legs are tiring, and when my head slips under I panic and flail my arms harder. I pop up. I can see the shore bobbing about twenty feet away until I slip under again, and then all I see is black water. I take two or three strokes without breathing and with a last bit of energy I kick and break water and take a huge lungful of air. And then I slip back under, my ears filling with the voices of loved ones.

I can't believe it's going to end this way, with me drowning in the Rio Bravo while trying to swim back into Mexico. As I start to slip under for good, I picture my bloated and unrecognizable body on the front page of a *nota roja*: *See How He Died Bringing Back Drug Money!* Of course, Papi would read it and think, good, one less smuggler, until he got to the part where the victim was named.

I picture Papi's eyes filling with tears, and the newspaper shaking in his hands, and when my feet sink a little more they surprise me by touching bottom. I stand, the water up to my shoulders, my whole body coming alive with relief. If there was a current it'd likely carry me away, but the river is slow and sludgy. I trudge toward land and crawl up a slippery embankment on my hands and knees. My spine arches as I gag up clear, slimy water. I'm breathing, though, the morning air rushing over the raw part of my throat. It feels like something's broken in there. Every time I swallow, I feel a thudding pain right in the middle of my windpipe. At least the knapsack is still on my back. I pull it off and look inside and see the money is still dry in the plastic bag.

Gracias a Dios, I think.

I sit and catch my breath and look across the river. The big man's still there, waving a fist in the air, his voice like a drone of mosquitoes. I start yelling back at him, the two of us having a shouting match across a brown rustling river, his voice strong with rage while mine sounds scratchy and worn. Then we quiet, and it's just the two of us looking at one another like we've run out of things to say. The whole thing is ridiculous—Mexico, the United States, what the two countries do to each other. All of it's a bad dream and it's like the militiaman and me are both waking up from it at the same time.

The man's shoulders slump and he suddenly looks tired. His nose and eye must hurt as much as my throat. He's breathing hard, looking at the water's edge, and I can tell he's thinking of going in and having a look for his gun. He paces the riverbank but then turns and walks back to his battered truck. From afar I watch him open the truck door. He climbs into the driver's seat and stares out the window, looking tired. Finally, I hear the engine start and I watch him drive off in a cloud of dust.

It's hot now, the sun at eight or nine o'clock in the sky. I call out, "*Hola!*" which causes a stab of pain in the middle of my throat. My croaky voice is swallowed instantly by the silence. It's the opposite of an echo; with nothing to bounce off, the sound waves wither in an instant, and then there's nothing but the sound of sand blowing across the desert.

I start walking along a path leading away from the riverbank. With nothing but wet socks on my feet, I can feel every little rock, pebble, and huisache needle. As the sun climbs higher in the sky, the ground heats up and soon I'm taking quick hopping steps so as not to burn the soles of my feet. It's impossible. The damp in my thin socks sizzles with each step, releasing puffs of awful steam. After a few hundred meters, I give up and sit in the shade thrown by a barrel cactus. There's nothing but desert scrub as far as I can see, and when the sun is directly overhead, there won't be any shade anywhere. My eyes smart and I take a slurp of water. Again, I call out, though this time the word is *help*. Nothing. Just wind. I try to walk a little more, until my burning feet force me to stop under the next bit of shade, thrown by the spindly branches of a half-dead paloverde. My heart is pounding and my head feels like someone or something is squeezing it.

I open the knapsack and dump the contents onto the path. All that's left is a bottle of water and a few tortillas and that plastic bag filled with cash. I upend the plastic bag and the bundles of money spill all over the desert floor. I pack them one by one into the knapsack, leaving the plastic bag behind. I tear the bag in two and double each piece around my feet. When I stand up, the heat's still there, but at least I can tolerate it.

I pick up the knapsack and put it back on and then I'm walking. I'd give anything for a hat. My lips are starting to crack and my throat still hurts every time I swallow. I keep taking little sips from the last bottle of water until only half of it's left. Now I'm afraid to drink it because I still have no idea how close I am to the road running parallel to the river.

Don't think.

Don't think about how thirsty you are.

Just walk.

I HEAR A HISS, though when I turn to look all I see is chip bags and scrub. I stand perfectly still for a moment, listening. I've heard stories of people dying from snakebites while crossing into America. Apparently your tongue swells and you can't breathe and when they find you your lips are blue. Just my luck it'd happen to me while trying to cross back into Mexico.

I start walking again. I can barely think, the sun's so hot. I finally give in and drink some water. Though it's warm enough to simmer an egg, it helps. I keep my eyes on the desert floor, on the lookout not just for snakes but also for broken Coke bottles and biting spiders and those burrowing crevices left by desert voles. As I grow tired, my head empties and in a way this is a good thing. I keep trudging forward until I hear the faint whine of a car tire on tarmac. I lift my head and sure enough, in the distance,

I see a car moving. I hurry my pace. The sand is still broiling my feet, and the sun is still broiling the top of my head, though it doesn't bother me as much. The road keeps getting closer and closer and once I'm there I'll be sure to flag down something. In Mexico no one ever passes by anyone who needs a ride without stopping.

Suddenly, I feel light, like there's air inside me, needing to float. I'm giddy, tearful. I can't believe I've done it. I'm like Ernesto when he came back from *his* first job for Tranquilo, bursting into the kitchen, laughing and singing and hugging Mami, and then he started spending money all over town, on stupid shit he didn't even need.

After about twenty minutes, a blue speck appears on the horizon, so far away it's shimmery and silent. Slowly it gets bigger. Soon I can hear belching exhaust and a straining motor. It's an early model Mazda pickup, coated in rust and patches of dull red body compound, the flatbed filled with men off to some job.

I don't even need to stick out my thumb.

"Nice shoes," says the driver with a wink. "You buy those on sale?"

"Can I get on?"

"Well, I don't know. You might make the others jealous with your footwear."

He nods toward the back and winks.

"*Gracias*," I say.

The two men closest to the broken-open tailgate each hold out a hand to haul me up. There are six workers in the back of the truck, and each one is gray with construction dust. They're all short and big around the chest, with lunch boxes at their feet.

For some reason, they don't tease me about the plastic around my feet.

"*Hola*," I say, and they all nod.

The wind rushes through my hair. I keep catching myself grinning. After an hour we reach Nuevo Laredo. We wind through busy, narrow streets filled with stray dogs and dirty-faced children. Women hold up trays of plastic bags filled with brightly colored drinks as we drive by. We pass electronics shops, clothing stores, and taco stands. When I notice a shoe store coming up, I bang on the side of the truck.

The driver pulls over. I hop out and walk up to the driver's window. "How much for the ride?"

"Are you kidding me? Spend it on some shoes!"

He drives off, honking the horn and giving me a thumbs-up. The men in the back barely notice I'm gone. It's mid-morning and I walk into the shoe store, which is empty except for some kids doodling in coloring books near the back. A salesman comes up to me. He's an older guy, his dark pants pulled high over his waist. He looks down at my feet, his thick eyebrows arching.

"Well," he says. "You've come to the right place, muchacho."

I pick out a pair of Nike sneakers. They're top of the line and I pay for them with the money in my knapsack.

"Nothing smaller than fifties?" he asks.

"No, sorry. My aunt gave me this money."

He nods and walks to the back of the store. When he returns he's got a handful of change, all of it in new pesos. The kids silently work away in the background. Before I leave, he motions for me to lean toward him.

"The next time you visit your aunt in Texas," he whispers,

"remember to put your shoes in your knapsack, *si*? That way, they won't fill with water and drown you ..."

I smile and offer my hand. His skin is warm and scratchy.

"Welcome home," he says.

"*Gracias*," I tell him, and outside I hail a taxi driven by a guy with tin teeth and a crucifix hanging from his rearview mirror. The steering wheel is wrapped in cloth, I guess so he won't burn his hands at midday, and as he drives away he taps his hands to the tinny polka music blasting from his stereo.

"Where to?" he asks, and I give him an address.

Ten minutes later, I'm ringing the buzzer at Tranquilo's house.

17

▲▽▲▽▲▽

THIS TIME, when Ramón comes out to meet me, he gives me one quick look and lets me in. I hand him the backpack and he walks off, assuming I'll follow him into the house. When I do, he points at one of the chairs and says, "Wait there."

I sit down. A woman is sitting on the sofa opposite me, flipping through a fashion magazine. She has dark hair and long legs and looks like Eva Longoria. She glances up at me and goes back to her magazine, which she doesn't really seem to be reading. She's just flipping pages with long nails lacquered red. I can smell her perfume wafting across the room.

There are four papered bricks on the coffee table in front of me, all of them bearing the Double-C stamp. I can hear the soft *whirr* of an air conditioner. The woman turns the pages of the magazine, and every so often she changes the tilt of her head from left to right.

I hear a door open. Though the woman doesn't look up from

her magazine, I turn and see Tranquilo coming toward me. As before, he's wearing dirty jeans, a torn ball cap, and that Rolex, weighing down his left wrist. As before, he's smiling—it's all his face can do—though it looks like there's an *extra* smile in there today, pushing the corners of his mouth up a little higher.

"So," he says in that soft voice of his. "Diego Hernandez. Or should I say … Hector Valdez?"

He laughs and bends over the sofa and kisses the beautiful woman. "Give us a few minutes, would you, *amor*? I've got to speak with Mr. Valdez here."

The woman stands and walks to the back of the house. Tranquilo sits next to the magazine she left behind.

"Congratulations, *cabrón*. You did it."

"All the money's there," I say. "Minus a tiny bit I needed for expenses. I'll pay that back as soon as I—"

"Nickels and dimes, amigo. Don't worry about it. The point is everyone's happy, *si*?"

I nod. He points at me.

"Since your car's gone and those are bruises around your neck, I'd say you ran into a few problems along the way."

"*Si*."

"And if I'm not mistaken, those aren't the same shoes you left in. Plus I can smell the Rio Bravo on you." He leans forward. Suddenly, I have to strain less to hear him. "That river has a smell, you know? Mud mixed with oil mixed with sweat. Plus blood. There's the blood of a thousand Mexicans in that river. You had to swim for it, didn't you?"

"*Si*, I'm sorry—"

"Sorry? Why sorry? You were just doing what you had to. Listen to me, muchacho. The first time's always a test. It's just the nature of the beast."

Tranquilo turns. Ramón appears and places a wad of bills, held together by a plastic band, on the coffee table next to the bricks of heroin. "You're looking at your commission, minus what your brother borrowed from me and what you spent at Saturn 400. There's still close to five thousand dollars there."

My heart skips.

"You earned it, *hijo*. You helped me out in a big way. Losing that tunnel—ay, what that did to me. You think it's easy building a half-decent tunnel? You need an architect, an army of diggers, houses at either end. Plus time. It's not a problem that'll go away soon."

Reaching out, I pick up the money, riffling the bills like they do in the movies. I can't believe it's all mine.

Tranquilo watches me. "I'm gonna ask you a question."

"Okay."

"And you're gonna think hard before you answer."

"I will."

"You want to do this again?" He nods at the drugs on the table. "You say yes and you'll start out debt free this time. Your cut would be worth about thirty thousand dollars."

My heart pounds against the wall of my chest. The thought of all that money makes me feel ill with excitement. I look at him, speechless.

"I know, I know, you don't wanna turn out like your brother. Don't worry. To tell you the truth, this drug business is a real pain in the *culo*. And I'm not talking about the police—most of them work for me already. It's the sort of people black tar attracts. Hot-heads. Attention seekers. Show-offs. Addicts. People like your brother."

He pauses, letting this sink in.

"Let me explain something else. We're moving into a new phase. The gringos call it diversification, and every company has to do it, sooner or later, if they want to stick around. Peppers, avocados, plantains, coffee beans, pineapples. Pretty soon we'll control the flow of these into *el norte* as well. And since my business is changing, my labor needs are changing too. I don't need gangsters anymore. What I need, Diego, is people like *you*."

I say nothing. None of this is making sense.

"Within ten years," he continues, "this little business of ours will be trading on the stock market. Maybe even the Dow. Of course, we'll have to call it something else. Something without the word 'cartel' in it. It's not right for the future. It was never our name anyway. People just started calling us the Double-C and it stuck. What I'm saying is this, Diego. You got a future with us. But until that happens"—he nods toward the bricks on the table—"there's our cash flow to think of. This package needs to be in San Antonio within the next two weeks. Again, Crazy J will get it. I've spoken with him and he's happy to have you again. Says you're the type don't attract attention. What do you think?"

I can't answer. Tranquilo holds up the palm of his hand. "Don't worry. I can give you some time to think this over. I'm not going to force you. That sort of thing never works in the long run. I had to learn that over and over till it finally sunk in. I'm not a smart man, Diego. Grade six was the last I saw of school. But I know how to get things done, you get me? Let me know in two days.

You say no, we never see each other again. Unless of course you change your mind. *Esta bien*, amigo?"

"*Si*," I croak.

"In that case, *hasta luego*. It's been a pleasure doing business with you."

RAMÓN WALKS ME TO THE DOOR AND, with a nod, shows me to the street. The steel mesh gate clangs behind me and I start walking toward the center of town. My head is a swirl. All it would take is a few more deliveries over the border and I'd be set for life. My thoughts turn to plans. With the five thousand dollars, I could get myself the plainest used car I could find, a Corolla or Chevy Impala. The sort of car no border guard would ever suspect. Then when I didn't need it anymore I could give it to Papi as a replacement for the Datsun I left behind in Texas.

I reach a busy street lined with stores and white-tile restaurants. The sidewalks are full of people and I can't stop thinking about the five thousand dollars in my pocket. It's like they all know and admire me for it. A *colectivo* chugs by. I wave it over and when the driver says he's heading west I get in. I'm sandwiched between two women with dark skin wearing peasant blouses, both of whom are taking live chickens to market. Ahead of me are some old *mestizos*, and they're sucking on the cheapest cigars on earth. The smoke wafts into my face, and while this ordinarily would have driven me mad, on this day it doesn't. In the third row are five kids, perhaps belonging to the two campesinas with the chickens. They're fighting and shrieking, and the littlest one is bawling away, tears forming tracks in the dirt on his face.

We drive along. The *colectivo* has an old clanking diesel engine and the cabin keeps filling with oily fumes. It's loud too. The two men in front of us shout to have a conversation. I smile. I can't help it; everything looks different. With one simple decision, my days as a *nini* could be over. With one simple decision, I could be a rich man.

The woman beside me notices.

"You're having a good day, *verdad, joven*?"

"You're right, I am, señora."

"Okay, good then. All days won't be this way."

WHEN WE APPROACH THE ROAD leading from the highway to Corazón, I tap on the roof and call out, "Señor!"

The driver pulls over and opens the *colectivo*'s front door with a long metal handle. I crawl past the other passengers, excusing myself when I accidentally step on a bag of handwoven dolls. As I struggle to get out, the kids never stop caterwauling and the men in the front never stop arguing. Football, they're talking about. At times, it's as if nothing else exists in Mexico.

I step into chilly air. It's turned dark, the sky a patchwork of wispy, gray-blue clouds. It's a gusty night. Somewhere far off a coydog howls, its cry picked up by the wind and swirled around so that, for a few seconds, it sounds like there's a pack of them, all upset. Then there's silence, except for the wind in my ears.

I walk toward the village and soon I'm passing the same low pink and blue adobe houses I've passed my entire life. I know who lives in every one, give or take a few. After another block I reach the town's smaller plaza, the one with the dried-up well in its center. Whatever happens, you won't catch me growing old and hanging my head into its depths, listening to my problems echo up from the mossy bottom.

I come to my family's house and let myself in. Everything's in shadow, with just a glimmer of moonlight through the windows. I sit on the sofa and remove my Nikes and stretch out, El Tranquilo's money still in my front right pocket.

I hear a rustle from the bedroom where my parents are sleeping. I look up and Papi's in the doorway of the living room, wearing underpants and a white cotton T-shirt. He has his usual expression, the one saying he understands nothing about the world he's suddenly found himself in. The truth is, he changed when Ernesto started paying the bills. It was like someone took the blood out of his veins. It was like the air left his lungs.

"Diego," he whispers. "You're back."

He sits in the chair facing the sofa. If he wonders where Ernesto's things are—the things I'd supposedly gone to Nuevo Laredo to collect—he doesn't ask. If he can see the bruising around my neck in the dimness of the room, he doesn't mention that, either. By tomorrow I'll have to make up a story. A disagreement with some toughs in the street. Yes, I'll get in trouble, but so what?

"How was your trip?" he asks in the quietest of voices.

"Papi," I whisper. "I have bad news."

"What's that, *hijo*?"

"Your car. It died just outside of Nuevo Laredo. I had to leave it. I'm sorry."

He shrugs. "That's okay."

"But you loved that car," I say. "You took Mami on your first date in that car."

He shrugs again. "It was a piece of crap, Diego. We both know that. When I'm working again I'll get a new one." He waves his hand in the air. "To tell you the truth I was sick of the damn thing."

There's a windup clock on the kitchen table. It ticks and ticks and ticks, and I feel like those ticks mean something, that everything about this moment I'm having with Papi has some importance I can't quite grasp.

His eyes flick up at me. He looks like he wants to ask me something, but is nervous about doing so.

"What is it, Papi?"

"It's just ..." He pauses. He's always had these big horse eyelashes, so big they seem to weight his eyelids. Mami says that's where I got mine.

He knows something's happened. He can barely get the question out. He fears what I might tell him. I can see it on his face. Ernesto once told me it's better to die young and rich than old and poor. I wonder if he could be right.

"It's just that ... on the phone you said you were going to look at the *colegio* in Nuevo. Did you do that, Diego?"

I take a deep breath. It's not easy lying to him. Mami, Ernesto —for some reason, I don't mind. But not him.

"*Sí.* I did. It was nice."

"You know I went to school there."

"*Sí.* I know that."

"Best years of my life."

I lower my eyes. I can't look at him. The ache in my throat deepens. When I was little I used to crawl up on him and stick my nose into his neck and just breathe. The problem is we're the same, he and I, and nothing's ever going to change that.

"Diego?"

"*Si*, Papi?"

"I'll see you in the morning. Don't stay up too late. You look tired."

He stands and walks back to the bedroom. I hear the walls groan where the hammock hooks are fastened. They creak for a few seconds and then stop when Papi's hammock comes to rest. I sit in darkness. In five weeks I'll be eighteen, and I would never have guessed there's a type of fatigue that seeps into the bones and makes them ache as if you had the flu. At the same time, I know that sleep won't come, at least not anytime soon. My eyes make out shapes in the gloom. Triangles and squares, mostly. And my ears! They've never been so alive. It must feel this way to be crazy, every noise as loud as every other noise. There's the tap dripping and the refrigerator churning away and Mami muttering in her sleep. From outside comes the sound of wind blowing and our chickens clucking and then there's the drone of cicadas, an electric buzz that never goes away, at least not here in the north of Mexico. They're all the sounds of my life, and tonight, at least, they muddle any thoughts of a new one.